The Bodyguard

Undercover Series Book 1

Ruchi Singh

ISBN 9798886291070

THE BODYGUARD

Undercover Series

Book 1

By

Ruchi Singh

To

my son

Jayesh

PART ONE:PRELUDE

October 1st

He had been *following Vikramaditya Seth Jr. for years. Watching, and waiting. Patiently. Tenaciously. Not a tough task since it was a conscious decision.*

He knew everything about Seth Jr.—the residences, offices, cars, relatives, and friends. The only hitch in his plan was Seth's routine, which was as unpredictable as the National Stock Exchange index.

Seth Jr. liked to be in his office early in the morning, but the timing was never the same. The choice of conveyance, by land or air, always varied with no fixed pattern. The guards sanitized the meeting venues and locations like he was the POTUS. Even the dates with the numerous lady-friends were unplanned. It never failed to amaze one at the way women readily fell in line with his erratic schedule.

The blame, or credit, for the unpredictability lay on that devious Nikhil Mahajan, Seth's security-in-charge, his right-hand-man, and a smart, arrogant sonofabitch.

He smirked at the thought. He liked smart sonofabitches. They gave him the opportunity to outsmart them. And today he was confident he would beat Mahajan, for he had changed his strategy. Instead of focusing on Seth, he had begun to concentrate on the people around Seth. Predictable beings. Predictable, boring beings like Sunil Baggah, a businessman.

Baggah always had Sunday lunch at Delhi Golf Club's open-air restaurant, at one p.m., at table number seven. And today Baggah had invited Seth there.

He looked at his wristwatch. A few more minutes of waiting left.

Taking his eyes off the viewfinder, he studied his surroundings. The green belt next to the golf course, maintained by the horticulture department, was like a mini-forest, devoid of all life except for the usual chirping birds and scurrying squirrels. Lush mint-green trees bathed in last night's downpour swayed in rhythm to the gentle breeze. The afternoon sunshine sieved through the canopy of thick leaves, casting a warm glow inside the thicket. It was a perfect day.

The wide branches of the Banyan tree he was perched on gave him adequate cover from anyone paying attention from the golf course. He had had the place under surveillance for the past one month and was confident of no human interruptions or surprises. Yesterday's rain had given him a sleepless night, but today the skies were as clear as they could get. He took it as a divine blessing from Maa Kaali.

An imperceptible movement brought his gaze to the nearby branch. A chameleon sat like a carved statue merging with the ebony brown of the bark. Excited at the chance of a little sport, he reached slowly towards his feet and took out the knife from the case strapped to his boot. Without taking his eyes off the creature, he struck out in one clean sweep.

Khatchak!

Wriggling, the upper half of the chameleon fell to the ground. Blood poured out from the remaining half still glued to the branch, stunned into a stupor. The red liquid oozing out of an animal always surprised him. Shouldn't the color be different from us humans? He nudged the half-carcass down with the knife's tip and wiped the blade on the bark before sheathing it inside its leather cover.

Rejuvenated by the sport, he inhaled the fresh air. The faint misty mud-fragrance rising from the wet ground reminded him of a distant childhood memory when he had lifted a stone in the park where he played and seen earthworms crawling underneath. He had enjoyed smashing each one of them with the stone. They didn't have red blood in them, he remembered and sighed. Fingering the rudraksh string around his neck, he blanked his mind and focused on the task ahead.

He had a clear view of the white wicker tables set inside the boundary of the golf course, just shy of a thousand yards from his location. Once the men were seated at the table, the multi-colored garden umbrellas would cease to matter for an uninterrupted line of sight. Though the direction of the wind was perfect, he was concerned about the speed. But then it would be no fun if there was no challenge.

Mentally revising the exit route one more time, he looked back and located his car beyond the woods—a nondescript white Tata Indica, which he would ditch at a pre-planned location and hire a public transport.

Assured, he looked around again. Not a single soul stirred in the region. Had the squirrels gone for their siesta or had they sensed his intent? Even the chirping birds had gone quiet in-sync with their cohabitants. Was it time for action? He glanced towards the cluster of tables, his karmabhoomi, and frowned.

Two golf carts stood on the paved pathway near the tables. Were they early? Maybe by a few minutes. It didn't *bother him. He checked the flash-sound-suppressor of his .338 Magnum, aligned the scope, aimed the cross-hair at table number seven, and positioned his trigger-finger.*

It was time to end the long wait.

Maa Kaali had waited long enough for the bali. And a fitting sacrifice she would get.

'Om Krim Kaaliaaye Namah!'

GOLF CLUB ENTRANCE
1ST OCTOBER, 12:45 PM

"Madam, change," the auto-rickshaw driver shouted, handing out a five-rupee coin.

"Keep it," Esha said, jumping out of the vehicle.

Anxious about the outcome of her interview, she absentmindedly signed the visitors' register at Delhi Golf Club's entrance gate. The guard directed her towards the open-air restaurant, where she was meeting someone for a job opening. Her savings were dwindling fast, and she was desperate.

Walking on the paved path, as she did a last-minute check on her resume and certificates in the file, she rammed into someone. "Goddamn!" The file and papers flew out of her hand as she lost her footing and tumbled backward.

"Steady..." Hard, confident hands held her shoulders as she tried fielding the scattering papers, pen, and file.

Flustered, she looked up at the familiar yet elusive face. Hooded eyes, partially visible behind the steel-grey shades perched on a sharp nose, looked straight into hers. Something traversed down to her toes, something strong, something powerful. An acute self-awareness overcame her and the apology died on her lips.

The only response she got for her tongue-tied stare was a knowing, slight upward movement of one corner of his mouth. Contrary to her nature, the pounding heartbeat for a complete stranger baffled her. But before the recognition dawned that she had crashed into the legendary industrialist Vikramaditya Seth Jr., his security retinue swept her aside gently and ushered him towards the open-air restaurant.

Watching him walk away, she recalled how the media had gone gaga over him when he had taken command of Seth Industries after his father's death earlier this year. A prodigy, with an exceptionally high IQ and command over no less than four languages, he was professed to be a brilliant strategist with a farsighted vision. Yesterday, she recalled watching a small clip of news showing his presence in Delhi in relation to a mega-infrastructure project in Myanmar.

Her heart thudded again when, without breaking his stride, he turned and glanced at her. She wasn't sure if she felt hot because of her blazer or him.

Not willing to give him an upper hand——for the second time—she held the eye contact, lifted her chin and schooled her face to present the blank, poker expression she was famous for until he and his entourage moved out of her sight.

GOLF CLUB RESTAURANT
1ST OCTOBER, 12:50 PM

Vikramaditya Seth didn't have the patience for whining complainers, even if one was an intelligent, whining complainer. Throughout their pathetic game of golf, which Sunil Baggah didn't know how to play, he had gabbed on and on about fictitious people threatening him because of the contract they were to sign soon. Even Nikhil, following them, had begun rolling his eyes and coughing suggestively. Scared to the core, Baggah told them that he had filed an FIR asking for additional police protection.

"If you want to back out, now is the time, Sunil. I won't mind," Vikram said, standing at the restaurant table reserved in Baggah's name.

"No... no... Vikram. You know I'm no coward." Baggah pulled a chair.

'No, you are a greedy coward.' Vikram sighed and gestured to Nikhil to take a seat at the table, but as always Nikhil refused and positioned himself right behind Vikram's chair, scanning the surroundings.

"Mahajan, you should relax... have a salad or a drink." Baggah opened the menu card.

Nikhil refused again. The guy was so obsessed with Vikram's security that it sometimes got onto Vikram's nerves too.

Baggah continued. "No one will have the courage to take on the mighty Vikram Seth in broad daylight. It is us—mere mortals—people down below the chain who have to be..."

Tuning-off Baggah's monotonous nattering, Vikram studied the white picket fenced restaurant and the gardens. The area was huge, a typical characteristic of Delhi clubs. The green lawns looked beautiful under the balmy sun. He sighed again. How he wished he could enjoy the spectacular day without the ever-nagging business discussions, and partners like Baggah eating up his time! Just him, a glass of rum... alone or perhaps with a partner who would understand and want him the way he was—moody, short-tempered, overbearing. Adjectives attributed to him by his mother and ex-wife—not that he agreed with them.

When was the last time he had taken a vacation? He couldn't recall.

"So what would you like to have?"

Baggah's raspy drawl brought him back to the question of lunch. He glanced at the menu and grimaced at the same old continental cuisine. A sudden memory of yellow *tadka daal* with *ghee*-laden *rotis* and his father scolding him for not eating veggies caught him unawares. He wondered at his unusually emotional chain of thoughts. He really needed a break.

The crackle of a sizzler dish and the aroma of roasted onions, from the adjacent table, made him glance at the menu. He placed his order for the first course.

It must have rained last night, Vikram thought as he went back to admiring the surroundings. The green landscaped gardens appeared fresh and nude like... like the face of the girl who had bumped into him. It wasn't surprising that she tip-toed into his thoughts so smoothly. She was distinctive. With her dusky, clear skin devoid of any trace of makeup, and short hair curling around her face, she looked nothing like the women in his coterie of acquaintances. And those honey-brown, deep eyes. A sliver of primitive desire ran through his toes.

Her flabbergasted, tongue-tied response was nothing new. People reacted to him that way many a time. But even during those astonished, dumb moments, she exuded confidence and elegance from every aspect of her demeanor. He couldn't fathom what made him glance at her again earlier. She had recovered her composure and had met his glance squarely and confidently. Admirable. He wouldn't mind her with him on his dream holiday. And, of course, the glass of rum on the rocks.

He did a double take when the woman occupying his mind entered the restaurant area and scanned the tables. He frowned. Was she looking for him? Looking to further their two-second acquaintance? His lips contorted in distaste. Perhaps the collision wasn't as innocent as he had been made to believe. But her reaction looked too natural and genuine to be pre-meditated. Maybe she was an actress.

No one could blame him for mistrusting women. The fairer-sex had fallen for him left-right-center throughout his life, even when he was married.

Bringing his gaze to the menu card in his hand, he waited for her to seek him out, gasp and approach him with feigned familiarity. He scowled when, after a few seconds, he heard no breathless greeting. He glanced up to find her marching to a table to his left, lean and lithe clad in a navy blue blazer and grey trousers, completely oblivious of his presence. A middle-aged bald man stood up at the table she was headed towards.

As she walked behind Vikram's chair something hit his elbow knocking the menu card off his hand, and something heavy dropped down on his left with a thump.

"Ah…"

Hearing the muffled groan, Vikram turned to see her sprawled on the ground. He bent down to help her. Baggah stood up shouting.

Then all hell broke loose!

Everything happened at once. One moment, Baggah was yelling. The next moment, he went quiet and fell face-down on the table. Someone gasped. His hand, outstretched to help the woman, shook and his heart slammed against the ribcage. Nikhil shouted. Vikram heard a faint whistle. His chair jerked. White cotton stuffing flew all over. The back cushion of Vikram's chair had been ripped apart.

Screaming and bellowing instructions to the guards, Nikhil pushed Vikram down. His head rammed into the fallen girl's stomach. She gasped and grunted again. After a second of stunned silence, she wriggled out from under his weight and moved towards Baggah. The pristine white tablecloth had turned red under Baggah's chest.

As the waiters and the club guards converged towards their table, Nikhil pulled Vikram up and steered him out of the restaurant. Vikram glanced back and saw the girl, in the blue blazer, sprinting like a gazelle towards the massive green Banyan grove near the barbed wire fence of the Golf Club.

POLICE STATION, NEW DELHI
1ST OCTOBER, 6:00PM

"Ms. Sinha, what were you doing at the club?" The pot-bellied sub-inspector thumped the scarred, rickety wooden table with his fist, after his boss, the senior inspector, had left.

The young officer standing beside Esha cringed at the sudden noise. A recruit, she guessed. The lady constable standing in one corner, least bothered about the discussion or the situation, nibbled on the nails of her right hand.

Good thinking by them that they had stationed the woman or Esha would have added one more charge to her list of complaints that she was determined to file against the police after her release.

The sub-inspector repeated the question. Sitting straight on the hard iron chair, she ignored the pain in her hip and unflinchingly met the sub-inspector's gaze. His nostrils flared and trembled all the more at her blank stare.

The guards at the Golf Club had detained her after the violent incident and had confiscated her mobile phone. Later, the police had brought her to the station and had been interrogating her for the past three hours. They didn't allow her to contact anyone. She wasn't worried though, her family was only interested in the pay-check she brought.

Ignoring the sub-inspector glaring at her, she looked around the dingy, dusty cell in the police station. The bulb hanging from the high ceiling threw pale golden shadows all over, not doing anything for the dismal ambience of the room. The offensive stench drifting from the small round ventilator, high up on the back wall, indicated that the urinals were next to the lock-up—a deliberate ploy to weaken the fainthearted. But what they refused to believe was that she was not some common criminal or an ordinary female.

"Ma'am please, tell us the truth. It is in your interest." The young officer stepped towards her, playing the part of good cop to perfection.

"I've already told you everything," she answered, just to ease his distress.

The senior inspector had asked the same question several times before someone called him away. The bruise on her cheek throbbed, along with the anger she felt at the fools. Besides the knock on her hip, her midriff ached when she took deep breaths. Her ribs had probably taken a blow when the man fell on her. On top of all this, she had eaten nothing after breakfast. Her stomach grumbled in agreement.

For once, she cursed her habit of taking charge of a situation that was not her responsibility. But years of training had kicked in the moment she saw blood when the other man had keeled over. Trying to estimate the direction of the bullet and running towards the woods was a wrong move. They believed her to be an accomplice, whereas she had acted on impulse the moment she had realized the direction from where the shots were fired and had gone after the culprit. She had scanned the woods but hadn't seen anything or anyone. Some unknown force had stopped her before she could climb the fence, or it would have been really incriminating for her.

"Who sent you there?"

Esha stared at her hands. They hadn't put handcuffs on her wrists.

The lady constable fidgeted, shifting her weight on her left foot and began the mouth-manicure of the other hand. At this rate, she wouldn't be left with any nails, Esha thought, but couldn't blame her for the boredom. The woman had not budged from her position since the time Esha had been brought into the police lock-up.

"Whom are you working with? Why did you run towards the woods? Who was there?" With each question, the sub-inspector stabbed the scarred wooden desk with his flimsy pen. The tip broke at the final question.

Esha glanced at him, taking in the scowling gaze, fisted hands and sweating arm-pits. His condescending attitude was getting on her nerves.

"Am I under arrest? Do you have a warrant? If yes, I need a lawyer and if not, then you cannot detain me."

"So you will teach me the law? Will you... you bitch?" The fatso sneered. "Why were you there? Whom are you working for?"

"Ma'am please..." The other officer appeared genuinely embarrassed at the insult the fat sub-inspector had hurled at her.

She exhaled, knowing that rubbing them the wrong way would not go well for her under the circumstances. "I'm not working for anyone. I went there for a job interview. I would request you to talk to Mr. Singhal. He had fixed the meeting well in advance."

"Why did you detain Mr. Seth when he was entering the restaurant?"

"I didn't! I told you he came in my way. Listen, at least check my credentials with—"

The door of the cell opened, screeching ominously, and the inspector, who had made her life hell for the first two hours of the interrogation, entered the dusty room. The sub-inspector stood up deferentially and made way for him. Not meeting her eyes, the inspector glanced sheepishly at his team members and said, "I apologize for detaining you, Ms. Sinha. Here is your phone. You are free to go, but Mr. Kaul would like to have a word with you before you leave."

Esha wasn't surprised on hearing the name. She had reported to DIG Kaul for a brief period of time during her service. Though the delay was unexpected, she had been waiting for his intervention the moment she had given her credentials to the police.

The sub-inspector did not meet her eyes as she left the lock-up.

⬥⬥⬥

HOTEL TAJ MAHAL, NEW DELHI
1ST OCTOBER, 8:00 PM

"Looks innocent enough... her foot got entangled in the chair and she fell. Her fall, kind of saved me..." Vikram replayed the grainy black and white CCTV footage of the incident for the third time in his suite at the Taj Mahal hotel. The video had been enlarged at some crucial places, distorting the resolution. "...though why she ran to the boundary wall is beyond me."

He squinted at the images and adjusted the laptop sitting on top of his notes on the study table for a better view. The cameras did not capture anything beyond the fence of the Golf Club, though the police had found an abandoned sniper rifle in the green-belt adjoining the club's boundary.

Baggah, hit by the first shot, was in the hospital undergoing surgery. He was critical, and the doctors were not very hopeful.

Nikhil studied the crime scene pictures left by the police ten minutes back. The dead chameleon cut precisely in two halves gave him goosebumps. What kind of a maniac could have done that? He shoved the pictures back in the yellow manila envelope and threw them on the coffee table.

"I have a bad feeling about this, Vikram. I've called Uday into this and I think you should go back to Mumbai immediately." Nikhil handed Vikram his drink from the room's well-stocked bar. The snacks trolley they had ordered an hour back stood near the table, forgotten in the flurry of phone calls from family, friends, and police officials.

"Not again! We have had this discussion a number of times, Nick. I'll go as scheduled, after the dinner meeting tomorrow. Have to tie up a few loose ends of the Myanmar deal. No crazy gun-toting person can make me hide in a cave. If I do, they win." Vikram paused the video when he didn't get a response from Nikhil and glanced back, craning his neck. Nikhil stood behind him, massaging his jaw, eyes intent on something above the screen. "Nick?"

"Hmm... I was just thinking..."

"What?"

"What if Baggah hadn't stood up?"

"He would have received the bullet on his head instead of the chest. He was being threatened for quite some time—"

"So are you. Remember the IB report on the Myanmar project you are investing in?"

"Hah... that's hogwash... rebels in Myanmar don't have enough funds to operate in their own country, leave aside planning an assassination attempt on me here in India." He lit a cigarette.

"Then why the second bullet?"

Vikram took a deep drag. In all probability, he was the target, but he didn't want to attach more importance to the incident in front of his family and Nick till the time the investigations revealed the entire picture. Adding to their worry and anxiety with unnecessary attention would not help anyone.

"I have no idea, Nick." He tapped the cigarette over the ashtray. "Let's wait for the detailed reports from Uday and the police. Tighten the security, I don't mind, but don't ask me to stop work. If I agree to all your precautions, I'll end up sitting inside a bunker room with three exits, playing Poker with you." He smiled to take out the sting that had crept into his tone.

Nikhil, as usual, indifferent to his requirement of striking the right balance between security and freedom, continued to stare at something outside the window. He was a loyal friend, a fierce bodyguard, and a dedicated chauffeur all rolled into one. Vikram could never thank God enough for his friendship, even if the man was a paranoid sonofabitch. He chuckled silently.

It had all started that winter years ago when he had met Nikhil on a treacherous Kangari Mountain trek in Ladakh. The guide had paired them for the duration of the trek. In addition to sharing the tent, they found themselves sharing many a thing as young men in their twenties. He had loved Nikhil's down-to-earth attitude, more so since the latter was completely oblivious to Vikram's status and family fame. That winter was the beginning of a lifelong friendship and a deep bond between them.

Seven days into the trek, when they were returning, Nikhil's rope broke. He slipped on the incline and toppled over. It was Vikram's quick reflexes that had saved him. Catching hold of Nikhil's jacket belt, Vikram had hauled him to safety by sheer willpower. In the process, Vikram had dislocated a shoulder and cracked a couple of ribs, but had earned Nikhil's priceless loyalty.

After that near meeting with God, Nikhil had become Vikram's devoted slave. He closed his private investigation agency and joined Vikram as his round-the-clock personal bodyguard-cum-chauffeur. Heading the security department of Seth Industries, he took care of the personal security for Vikram's mother, too. He was as dedicated as humanly possible, so much so that Vikram had to force him to take a break once in a while.

"Tighten the security. Yes—" Nikhil broke off as his cell phone rang and took the call. "Mahajan speaking... yes. Ah yes... okay... really? This is surprising. Yes, of course, I'd like to thank her personally. Thank you. And Mr. Kaul, I request you to keep the lid on Major Sinha's identity... er yes, thank you." He disconnected and looked at Vikram. "Your savior is a decorated ex-army officer.

Major Esha Sinha, NSG trained black cat commando, one of the few ladies to have successfully completed the training and having five years of classified service under her belt. She has been given a clean chit. No wonder she assessed the situation so fast."

"No wonder..." Something clicked in Vikram's mind like a jigsaw puzzle falling in place—the posture, the alert, intelligent eyes, and the dash to the boundary fence.

"She had come there for an interview for some position in a security firm," Nikhil continued. "Though she has given her statement to the police, I wanted to hear a firsthand account of events from her point of view. I have asked Kaul to request her to meet us today, if that's possible. Would you like to be present?"

"Yes, of course." Vikram was surprised not just at his quick response, but also at the potent desire to see her again.

━━◆◆◆━━

Esha reached the Taj and scanned the lobby. The reception area was brimming with policemen, both in uniform and in plainclothes. She tried hard, but couldn't locate anyone who would fit the impression she had of Nikhil Kumar Mahajan.

Contrary to her nature, she was rapidly losing patience with the mess she had been involved just by being at a place at an inopportune time. Now she had been requested—nearly ordered—to go to the Taj Mahal hotel. Though DIG Kaul had apologized on behalf of the police department, he had commanded her to meet Mr. Seth's security in-charge the same evening. He had even arranged for a police vehicle and a driver.

"Major Sinha," someone called from her left.

She turned. It was due to her years of army training that she managed to mask her surprise at the handsome, well-built man in blue jeans and a black t-shirt smiling at her. As the personal bodyguard responsible for every moment of Vikramaditya Seth's life, she had assumed Mahajan to be an aging, nondescript man, and was ill-prepared for a taller and leaner version of actor Salman Khan.

"Major Sinha? Nikhil Mahajan." He scowled when he spotted her bruise. "You are hurt!"

"It's nothing. Esha Sinha." She took the hand he extended.

He gave her hand a firm shake and moved towards the lifts, oblivious of the admiring attention from a couple of girls and an old lady on the way.

"I'm so sorry you had to go through so much trouble. If circumstances had permitted, I'd have come to meet you personally, but I can't leave Vikram's side at all, certainly not after this afternoon's incident."

Slightly taken aback with his affability, Esha nodded and brushed away the apology with a wave of her hand as they entered the lift. The gratefulness of people always embarrassed her. She always thought of it as her duty, something she had been trained to do. Protecting civilians was second nature to her. A habit she was trying hard to break since after retirement she had no authority to take the law in her hands.

"I wanted to seek your opinion on the incident before we leave Delhi and Vikram wanted to thank you for saving his life."

That did it—her hands and toes went cold on hearing the name. She rubbed her hands on her trousers, unable to understand her juvenile reaction to someone who, up till now, existed just in newspapers and on television channels. She had been associated with many famous people and high profile dignitaries but had never experienced this strange nervousness at the thought of meeting someone. Clamping down the urge to turn around and leave, she checked her mobile for distraction.

"I hope you don't have any firearm?" Mahajan enquired as they exited the lift and nodded at the plainclothes man stationed at a door to their left. "I'm sorry I'll have to follow the regular security protocol."

"No issues." She held up her hands.

Mahajan frisked her impersonally, then swiped the magnetic card, and pushed open the door on the right— one which didn't have a guard posted. She wouldn't have been surprised if they told her that they had booked the entire floor of the hotel.

She sensed Seth the moment they stepped inside the room. To her brief reprieve, he stood looking at a file on the desk, talking to someone on his mobile. The smell of tobacco assaulted her almost immediately, causing her to take shallow breaths. Frowning, she scanned the room and found him holding a half-length glowing stub with the ash falling on the expensive carpet. He smoked!

Like Mahajan, he had also changed into a pair of jeans and a polo t-shirt—while the security-aide was in black, he wore a light shade of grey. Though shorter than Mahajan by a couple of inches, he was more muscular. Both men had a rugged charm that might appeal to the opposite sex, but not to her, she reiterated the thought silently. Then why in God's name was she comparing two men she had no business with? She mentally smacked her head.

"If you don't mind, could you describe the whole incident from your point of view?" Moving towards the recessed living area, Mahajan interrupted her chain of thoughts and gestured for her to sit.

Shutting the men and the smoke out of her mind, she began narrating the incident, trying to recall even minuscule details. Starting from the time she entered the restaurant, she told him about her fall and her move towards Baggah to assess the direction of the shot and the likely location of the sniper.

"You could have been shot," Nikhil said.

"Highly unlikely. I wasn't the target. An assassin never stays at his location after taking down the target—he just runs. The two shots were taken one after the other, one that hit the man and the other hit Mr. Seth's chair. After that there were none. It took me at least five to eight seconds to get up. He might have run away during that time." She suppressed the urge to rub her nose. "If you don't mind, may I see the video footage?"

"By all means." Mahajan pulled the laptop towards her and played the video.

She sat watching the whole incident, replaying it.

"So, what's the verdict?"

Vikram Seth's deep baritone cut through her calm speculations and her heart expanded in her chest. Her ribs throbbed in protest at her need for more air. She raised her glance and found him towering over them with that same unconcerned smile. But her attention was drawn to the scar on his right cheek, running below his ear and ending at the chin, making him a normal flesh and blood man instead of a larger-than-life film star as projected by the paparazzi.

"I think first of all you should thank Major Sinha for saving your life," Mahajan interrupted.

She was surprised at his friendly tone that had the slightest trace of admonition, quite unusual for a mere employee. Maybe their association was more than that of an employee and his employer.

"Inadvertently," she insisted, unwilling to establish any sort of connection with Seth. She had to stand up since Seth had extended his hand for a greeting.

His warm hand enveloped her cold one. "Inadvertently or accidentally, you did save my life Ms... er... Major Sinha. What happened to your face?" His eyes locked onto her face as if she was the center of his universe and nothing was more important to him than her.

"T's nothing."

"You are hurt." Instead of releasing her hand, he pulled her to the sofa and sat beside her. "Nick, why don't you hand me the first-aid box? It must be in the washroom cabinet." Releasing her hand, he took out another cigarette. Her nose began twitching.

"T's nothing," she insisted, as Mahajan went to do his bidding.

"You must have been hurting a lot, I remember my head rammed into your stomach when Nick, the idiot, pushed me down." He lit the cigarette.

"I'm good." Esha tried to shift further away on the sofa, but there was no space and she was already on the edge of the seat.

A ringtone broke the silence in the room. Mahajan handed Seth the first-aid box and moved to the balcony with his mobile phone.

Her gaze flickered from Seth to her watch and then back to him. "Should be going." Get a grip, she chided herself, she was thirty, not thirteen.

"What's the hurry? Someone's waiting for you at home?" Seth opened the box and examined the contents.

She scowled. Was it a deliberate reference to her relationship status or just an innocent question?

"They have an off-the-shelf ointment here. But first, we need to clean it, right?"

"I really don't need anything, it's a minor bruise." Esha stood up ignoring her aching muscles when he picked up a cotton swab.

What was he playing at, behaving like a perfect host in a hotel to a virtual stranger? Shouldn't they be discussing the shooting? He had been shot at in the afternoon and, instead of treating the incident seriously, he was brushing it away like a minor mishap. Maybe he was in denial. Or maybe he didn't trust the observation of a woman. She tightened her lips as the thought invaded her mind. From her point of view, it was wise and professional to come back to the disturbing topic of the shooting.

She cleared her mind, locked her hands behind her back and stated clearly. "I think you should look for a reason or motive for someone to harm you. In my opinion, the bullets were aimed at you."

His eyebrows went up as he scanned her from head to toe, taking in her rigid stance. "You think so?" A corner of his mouth lifted in amusement.

"I don't think so, I'm sure." Her hands fisted behind her back.

"How can you be so sure?"

"I have been trained to assess situations like this one."

"Baggah was not the target?"

"The elaborate way this has been executed—both the sniper and the rifle had to be top class to shoot from such a distance—shows that this was a highly paid or a resourceful and skilled assassin. If I were assigned to kill Baggah, I would have used a motorcycle, shot him at point blank and driven away. He doesn't have the protection you have. Then there is the question of the second bullet. If the target was Baggah, there was no need to fire a second shot."

Vikram Seth sat there staring at her lips, and she knew he had just then noticed her lisp, a speech impediment she had since childhood, a minor movement of her tongue touching her front teeth on certain sounds. She had tried hard to overcome it, but it was noticeable when she spoke at length.

"Mr. Seth?"

To her acute irritation, he chuckled. "You would have killed Baggah just like that?"

"Mr. Seth, I'd like to take your leave."

"I have offended you."

"I have absolutely nothing to lose if you choose to ignore my observations."

"Are you trained to be polite as well? Why don't you tell me to fuck-off? I know you are dying to say that. Come on… say it. You'll feel good."

"Fine, Mr. Seth. You may… … fuck-off."

He grinned, displaying a carefree boyish charm this time. She raised her eyebrows but it had no effect on him.

"Now that we are done with the official debriefing, why don't you sit and relax? Let's clean your wound and eat." Vikram Seth suggested, placing the first-aid box on the table. He pulled the snacks trolley towards him and lifted the dish cover.

"I don't—"

"Vikram, you just can't—"

She was astonished to see Mahajan, who had concluded his call, looking daggers at Seth.

"We'll discuss this when we get back to Mumbai, Nick."

"When will you pay attention to—"

Vikram dropped the cover back on the bowl and it cling-clanged loudly in the silent room. All of a sudden, the temperature in the room dropped.

In a fraction of a second, Esha saw him change from a mere friend to a rigid force to be reckoned with. Both men glared at each other. To give Mahajan some credit, he didn't back down either and matched Seth's penetrating angry glance with his own.

It was time for her to leave. "If you don't have any more questions…"

"Thank you, Major," Mahajan said.

"I'm indebted to you for life. Do let me know if I can do anything for you, ever," Seth shook her hand again but his mind was elsewhere.

Nikhil Mahajan, mercifully, escorted her out of the room. Her nose had begun to run. She gave in to the sneezes when she was alone in the lift. After a consecutive bout of ten, she took a few deep cleansing breaths to literally disassociate herself from the smoke and the man for good.

⚜

NIZAMUDDIN RAILWAY STATION, NEW DELHI
1ST OCTOBER, 8:00 PM

The railway station buzzed with travelers and their relatives who had come to see the passengers off. The lady in front of him struggled with her numerous bags and suitcases. He grimaced at the delay, skirted around her, and stowed his backpack on the x-ray machine.

He traveled light and considered getting attached to materialistic things a sign of weakness. But he too was weak, as far as certain things were concerned. The thought of the sniper rifle that he had to leave behind in the woods brought an instant pang of anguish and loss. He loved his guns and was proud of his collection in the basement of his house in Mumbai. At times, he longed to show them off to his few so-called cronies and acquaintances, but it would not be prudent to boast of an unlicensed collection. Somewhere, sometime, people would always tattle. Oh yes, complete detachment was tough.

Touching the holy beads on his neck, he moved towards the general compartment. The woman with the countless bangles threw an appreciative, lingering glance at him. Disgusted, he averted his face and moved forward.

He shook his head. If she knew... if only she knew, she would run the other way. Maybe one day, once this Seth business was over, he might take up one of these lustful women and tell the truth about himself. He would love to see the fear in their eyes when he would smash or tear their limbs one at a time. Would they still find him sexy? Would they still want him to be their toy boy?

These small fantasies brought him extreme pleasure, but his priority was something else right now. He could not afford to lose his focus. Seth was his one and only mission. He still had no news about Seth and Mahajan's reactions. What did they think about the shooting? Did they think Baggah was the target? Or were they suspecting that the attack was on Seth himself? He had no way to know the reaction of Seth's family members at the moment.

It could be taken as either a good sign or a bad one. He knew Seth had refused the Z-level security offered to him by the government on account of threats from the Myanmar rebels. Maybe they would think that the rebels had orchestrated this attack. But if Mahajan beefed up his security, it would be an added problem. He sighed.

Today's failure had made the game all the more complex. Involuntarily, his right hand went over his left arm. He had complete confidence in his years of sacrifice and devotion.

'Om Krim Kaaliaaye Namah!'

October 2nd

To Vikram's relief, his cavalcade of cars arrived home in time for a light dinner and sleep. He had almost dozed off while talking to his CFO over the phone on the plane.

The adrenaline rush from the shock of the incident at the club was receding. Baggah was out of surgery, but still critical. His wife and daughter's worried faces swam in front of Vikram's eyes. Vikram wanted to confront the man who had pulled the trigger and shake him until he received a satisfactory justification for the senseless bloodshed. No matter how much he pretended otherwise, the incident had stressed him out, and he just wanted to sleep. But it was not meant to be. At least, not for another hour or so. Though he had spoken with them right after the incident, his mother and elder sister stood at the door, waiting for him.

Plastering on a casual smile, he alighted from the BMW and took the steps leading to the Seth family's oldest residence—his home. He was amused at the contrasting images they portrayed. Vandana *di*, petite and gentle in a trouser suit, must have come straight from the office. Next to her, his mother, Meera Seth, stood tall and elegant in the ivory silk sari, a color that had become her trademark since his father died.

He nodded mechanically at the security staff bidding him goodnight as he took the three steps up the portico. *Di* anxiously inspected him from head to toe, whereas his mother tightened her lips as she glanced at him with disapproval etched on her graceful face. But she kept a hand on his head and gently ruffled his hair when he touched her feet. The tough exterior, he knew, was a facade for the world.

"Vikram! Are you all right?" *Di* stepped forward and gave him a warm hug.

"Not a scratch..." He spread his hand and grinned. He then glanced at their mother. "Why is my favorite person looking so grim? Erase this look, both of you... please. I'm fine." Vikram turned to hug his mother but did not receive the expected warm response from her rigid form.

"What did the police say? Did you engage Uday?" she asked instead.

"So glad to see you both, will you stay here today?" he asked, nodding to his mother.

"Vandana has to go back to Aaryan. He has his annual school function tomorrow, in case you have forgotten. But, I'll stay the night. Vandana, you should be on your way and take rest."

With a last concerned glance at him, *Di* sighed and moved towards the Range Rover parked in the driveway. The driver opened the rear door for her and whisked her out of the gate.

"Dinner?" his mother asked.

He nodded and followed her inside the house.

She took her place beside him on the dining table and served him the chilly-paneer curry. She did these small things whenever she stayed with him, bringing back childhood memories. In those days the conversation centered on his studies and hobbies. He would get no marks for guessing the topic of discussion today and braced himself for a long chat. Sleep had to wait.

"Sanghi *bhaisabh* had called about the threats from Myanmar. You have refused Z-security." She opened the conversation after Kishore *dada* served the *rotis* and retreated into the kitchen.

"Yes. He shouldn't have told you. This has nothing to do with the project. I'm pretty sure."

"You know I never interfere in the business, but this Myanmar project was the one deal I had told you not to pursue."

"Dad had given his word to the Head of the State." Vikram took a bite.

His mother exhaled. "And what about my wishes? Do I have a say in your life or not?"

"Of course you do, but this was one commitment I couldn't ignore. Our family's prestige is on the line."

"Ahh! The family's prestige... I don't know what else I'll have to sacrifice in the name of this family's honor." She tightened her lips when he frowned at her bitter tone. "Have they received the intelligence recently? What does the report say? How upset are the rebels, now that you have agreed to invest in their country?"

"The report is pretty thorough. The insurgents are not particularly fierce. And moreover, this attack was not from them. They haven't owned up to it." Vikram kept his fork down and patted her hand.

"Then who could have done this? Who could have such enmity with us? With you? I can't think of any—"

"Don't worry. It's under control. We have our own investigators working on the incident. Nick and I will beef up the security."

She frowned at her plate, not looking at him and not eating either.

"Mom?"

"Shall I tell you something?"

"Of course."

"I suspect someone killed your father."

His fork slipped and cluttered to the floor as his eyes jerked towards her. Kishore *dada* rushed in from the kitchen as quickly as his gout allowed. Concerned, he scanned the dining room and gave a fresh fork to Vikram at the subtle tilt of his mother's head.

"Kishore, please have your food and lock the doors. You can clear the table in the morning," she instructed. Their housekeeper-cum-chef of forty years nodded and withdrew.

"Mom, where did you get this idea from? It was a heart attack. The doctors confirmed."

"Nonsense! He was in perfect health. I know his blood pressure was a problem... but otherwise he was perfectly fine. There was no stress, nothing. This deal has done more damage to us than anything else."

"You are imagining things. He would have told me if there was any threat."

"Sometimes things are not the way they look, and despite all the precautions we take, things do happen... bad things..."

Now, he was concerned at her bleak and depressed tone. "Mom… when did you last meet Dr. Khurana?"

"Are you still going around with that girl, the lawyer?"

Taken aback with the sudden change in subject, he didn't reply for a few seconds and took another bite.

"Vikram?"

"Hmm…"

"Vikram, what Urvi did was a mistake. She's regretting it."

"Mom, we're divorced. It has been six months, the episode is over."

"Don't call marriage an episode! We had matched the horoscope, she was—is—perfect for you. Marriage is for keeps."

He exhaled and looked at her. "You are not aware of the whole mess, mom. Please drop it."

"Then tell me Vikram! Share with me. You are becoming more and more like your father. Obsessed about your work, businesses… and cynical about life. Have you ever thought about your personal life? Who are you working for? When your father was your age, we had had both of you. Vandana was eight and you were two."

He placed his hand on hers. "Mom, Aaryan is here. The current heir. He will manage everything."

"Aaryan! Aaryan? He is Jindal's son, not our blood."

"He is Vandana *di's* son as well. How can you say things like that, in these times?"

His mother opened her mouth to say something but didn't.

Vikram frowned. "I enjoy my work. It's not a burden. Moreover, I have not met anyone with whom I have any inclination of having kids. And chill, I'm not going to die. How can you get so perturbed because of a simple threat? We have always been under threat, from kidnappers, the underworld, politicians. This is also one of those things, and as I said, I'll follow all security protocols, mom."

"Life passes by and we don't even realize the folly of our decisions until it is too late."

"I think you are just feeling a little low. Shall I call Dr. Khurana?"

To his chagrin, she banged the spoon on the plate. "There is nothing wrong with me." She sighed and picked up the utensil again. "It's my fault. I've never questioned your father or you. Ever. So, when I do, you both infer I am not myself. I never interfered because I know you are busy and I didn't want to add to your tensions and worries. But I do want you to settle down. I want you to reconcile with Urvi."

"Mom, that's impossible." He picked up his fork again but the food was now cold and the paneer looked unappetizing.

❖

SUBURBS, MUMBAI
2ND OCTOBER, 9:00 PM

Entering his home, he dropped the backpack on a chair and switched on the only bulb in the room. A yellow glow fell on his possessions of nine years in the city—two easy chairs, a table, a folding bed against the far wall, and a small kitchenette with a mini-fridge on the side. Beside it was the door to an attached bath cum toilet in the corner.

He scanned the room carefully. Everything was in its place. The only window of the room was barred from inside with a heavy curtain draped over it. He had purchased this single-story house in a nondescript area of Mumbai when his sister had given him an advance after securing a job for herself. It had been expensive but a necessity.

He took off the rudraksh string and placed it in front of the statue at the altar he had made himself. He stood there for a minute, remembering his Creator, praying for justice and help in conquering the enemy.

Taking out a water bottle from the fridge, he drank straight from it, unmindful of stray drops sliding down his chin to the neck and onto his chest. The trip had been long and stressful.

The loss of opportunity had to be introspected, but he needed to steady his mind first. Letting disappointments get the better of him was a sign of weakness. But first things first. He'd have to take care of Sara.

She must be angry, very angry with him. He had never left her for two full nights at a stretch. Though he had arranged for the regular caretaker, she still must have missed him.

While preparing his dinner, he switched on the antique TV set for any news on the havoc he had created in Delhi. But there was absolutely nothing about the shooting at the Golf Club. What the heck!

Soon after, an advertisement blared along with the whistle of the pressure cooker. He flinched at the cacophony, lowered the volume and ran to switch off the stove.

The news bulletin resumed and the anchor covered his work. The same old news about shots being fired at the Golf Club and Sunil Baggah being critical was aired. But there was no news on Vikramaditya Seth Jr. The Seth family must have pulled some strings to silence the media.

The fact, however, was that he had been unsuccessful.

Sighing, he served the dinner on a plate and placed it on the tray along with her favorite dessert, gulab jamun. Balancing the tray carefully, he opened the double-door cupboard, drew the row of clothes hanging to one side, and pressed a lever on the panel, hidden by a long green overcoat. The plain wooden panel in front of him slid sideways to reveal a plush room. He reveled in the luxury that he could offer to his darling.

He had done up the room as Seth should have done for her, providing her with all the luxury the rich could buy. He had even built a small bathroom with waterproof plastic padding all over. The padding on the walls had been the difficult part to handle, but he had done it himself. The anxiety attacks made her restless and sometimes she wasn't able to control herself.

She lay on the recliner, hugging the plastic doll to her chest, wearing the same old suit, mended for the umpteenth time, watching TV. She threw a listless glance at him before continuing to watch the songs that he had programmed for her.

"Sara, dinner."

She didn't look at him again.

"Are you angry with me? I'm sorry I had to go, but it was only for a day."

She touched a finger to her lips, then patted the doll. "Don't disturb. It was difficult to put her to sleep today."

His heart wept at the picture she made, as he placed the tray on the small plastic table. Taking a spoonful of rice and lentils, he took it near her face. She dutifully opened her mouth.

"Will he come today?"

"No, I told you, he'll come tomorrow," he lied again.

She nodded and swallowed another spoonful.

Making sure that she had had her medicines after dinner, he left her sleeping with the doll tucked in its crib. The nightly ritual gave her the peace that she craved. Peace from her past, the betrayal—betrayal that was screaming for revenge. Her condition and her meek acceptance of her destiny gave strength to his resolve. He'll make them pay. No. There was only one left now. What a pity!

He'll get the divine justice, nonetheless. He deserved it. His Sara deserved it.

❦

October 3rd

Vikram looked up from his desk as someone opened the door without knocking.

"Here you go. The reports from the police." Nikhil tossed the reports in the yellow manila envelope, marked confidential in red, and flopped down on the sofa. The packet slid on the mahogany coffee table and fell at Vikram's feet.

"What are they saying?" Vikram picked up the envelope and placed it on the table. "I'm making a drink. What will you have?"

"The usual. As per the reports they have nothing to go on, but investigations are on. Uday and his team were there and he'll brief us tonight."

Vikram nodded and handed him a glass of Bourbon. "I have a feeling this is something else. Someone who wants to strike in the shadow of the Myanmar deal so that our suspicion is diverted."

"Maybe. But who could it be? Have you unnecessarily needled someone in the recent past?" Nick frowned as Vikram shook his head. "I cannot forget the neatly sliced chameleon at the Golf Club. I'm assigning Jay as chauffeur guard for your car since I won't be around all the time because of the investigations. I trust him blindly." Nikhil flipped the reports. "And am going to hire one more person to travel with you in the car along with the four guards who would follow you. What do you think?"

"I'm in your hands." Vikram shrugged and fired up his notebook. "Is the reference check for Maria's replacement complete? She'll go on leave in two weeks' time."

"Oh yes, Maria's replacement..." Putting his hands behind his head, Nikhil leaned back on the sofa, a slow smile appearing on his handsome face. "Why didn't I think of it earlier?"

Vikram looked up from his notebook and raised his eyebrows. "What?"

"I think it'll be fantastic. I have the perfect candidate in mind to replace Maria."

"What are you concocting now?" Vikram narrowed his eyes.

"What if we have another armed guard around you, in place of Maria?"

"A guard?"

"Undercover."

"One who will take minutes of the meeting and handle the P&L reports too?"

"Yes, she'll pretend she is taking minutes and handling reports."

"She?"

"She." Nikhil grinned as Vikram scowled. "What do you think about Major Esha Sinha? Will she do?"

"A woman? A bodyguard?"

"Careful, your gender bias is showing, boss." Nikhil grinned. "From what I've heard AND seen..." he winked at Vikram, "I'm quite impressed with her. I have her full details somewhere here..." He lunged to open his briefcase that never left his side and took out a file.

"You have a file on her! You have been thinking about it for quite some time, haven't you?"

"When you were talking business mumbo-jumbo with that fatso in Delhi, I was working. I wanted to recruit someone, so why not a woman? No one will suspect a woman." Nikhil opened a file. "Ah... here it is. She has recently retired from Short Service Commission. She is a crack shot, with a diploma in criminal psychology. She is one of the four women to be selected for the NSG since the time women have been allowed in the army. Though they never send women on a combat mission, she had been posted at the Indian embassy in France, as security aide to our Ambassadress for two years. She'll be the perfect cover."

"Wait a sec... what will she do in my office? What will I do with her?" Vikram spread his hands in the air.

"Looking at the diplomas and certificates in her name, I'm sure she must be intelligent. I'm confident that between the two of you, you'll manage to find a solution. No one will suspect. No one shall know this except the three of us."

"Pretend for sixteen hours in a day?"

"Office hours are about eight to nine hours. Only you work for sixteen hours. Come on... this is for only a few months until this blows over."

"You are assuming too much. She may not agree to take up the job."

"I'll give her an irresistible package. Moreover, who will refuse to work with the handsome, rich, and the most eligible bachelor of the century?"

"Don't employ her if she is single."

Nikhil flipped a few pages. "She is single. The more I think, the more I'm convinced about the idea that she is the best fit for the job. We'll forge the MBA degree for her to fit into the PA qualifications. She can be with you on your official meetings, luncheons, and dinners. I suggest we allow her to stay in the outhouse, the studio apartment above mine. And this, my friend..." Nikhil clinked his glass with Vikram's, "... will put you in the league of Gaddafi."

Vikram scoffed as Nikhil dialed a number from the file.

⸺⦁⊰⊹⦁⊹⊱⦁⸺

SETH TOWERS, MUMBAI
3RD OCTOBER, 9:00 PM

Uday, Nikhil's friend, and Seth's trusted private investigator since ages, entered the office to find Nikhil poring over the detailed reports he had received from the police, for the third time.

"Hey, take a seat," Nikhil said, barely looking up from the reports. "Vikram will join us soon, he's on a call. Help yourself." He waved towards the mini-bar behind the credenza as an afterthought.

Uday ignored his invitation for a drink and settled alongside Nikhil with his laptop.

"They found an abandoned white Indica in a mall's basement parking..." Uday began the moment Vikram joined them. Having known each other for a long time, the three of them shared an easy camaraderie. "No additional evidence in that car. No hair, no personal item, nothing left behind. He was well suited up."

"What about the car or its owner?" Nikhil asked picking up another report.

"Apparently it was stolen that morning from the office complex at ITO. He knew the car would not be missed for eight hours since the owner worked in the same building. It had been planned well in advance. He knew you would be there primarily because Baggah goes to the Golf Club every Sunday afternoon. The bastard had done his homework."

"What about the ballistics?" Nikhil asked.

"The shots matched the rifle left behind," Uday said.

"Who could it be?" Vikram paced the room. "I can't think of any incident or business deals where there could be an iota of enmity."

"I would suggest you get your financial records audited for any shareholder who has made a major loss in the past two years," Uday said. "Let's say anyone who has lost more than twenty lakhs."

"Okay."

"And now we need to look closer," Uday said, voicing the inevitable topic. He had his own conclusions since Seth Sr.'s death but wanted Vikram to think on those lines, else it would be difficult to convince him about the next steps.

"What do you mean?" Vikram stared at Uday.

"We need a motive. Who will stand to gain from your death? Let's start with Viraj. Last I knew he was not too happy with your grandfather's, and later his father's, will."

"Yeah, Vikram has controlling stake in the business he's managing. Their grandfather had left that stipulation because of Viraj's not-so-great business acumen." Nikhil sat down beside Uday.

"Viraj is a spineless man. He doesn't have the IQ or the resources to plan for such an elaborate attack." Uncomfortable with the thought of casting doubts on his own family members Vikram stood up to make a drink for himself. He knew Uday and Nikhil wouldn't let up until they had dissected each and every member of his family. He couldn't blame them as it was their job, and both were experts in their respective fields.

"Still, he needs to be put under surveillance," Uday said.

"Okay."

«Your ex-wife?»

"She doesn't get anything whether I'm alive or dead."

"Revenge could be a powerful motive," Uday said. "Woman scorned... blah, blah..."

Vikram chuckled. "Okay fine. Put her under surveillance too."

"Mr. Jindal?"

"He has enough money of his own," Vikram said.

"Elections do need lots of money on a continuous basis," Nikhil added.

"Aaryan?" Uday asked.

"Oh, come on... you are suspecting an eight-year-old?" Vikram threw his hands up in the air.

"No, but he is named in your will. Jindal stands to gain even if only as a trustee," Nikhil reminded him, "... and elections are expensive affairs."

"It'll be good if we get him and his affairs under our radar," Uday insisted.

"Fine, do it. But be discreet. And you both need to know, as per my will Jindal doesn't get the authority over my assets. I have divided the power of attorney between Vandana *di* and my mother." Vikram informed them, lighting a cigarette without taking their permission. *'To hell with manners.'* He knew what was coming.

Uday sighed to brace himself from the tsunami his next question would invoke, but someone had to bring up the subject. "So what about them?"

Vikram stared at him the way Uday had expected. If possible, Vikram's eyes would have drilled holes in his face.

"Money and power are the biggest motives," Uday didn't let up.

"And my mother and sister will hire someone to get me killed when they themselves are rich and powerful enough? Get some perspective, man."

"What's the harm in taking extra precautions?" Nikhil said.

Vikram slammed the glass down on the table. "They are not to be suspected and put under any kind of surveillance. And that's final." He stood up and stormed out of the room.

Nikhil sighed. "Okay, keep the lid on. In the public's eye we are treating this shooting as an attack on Baggah and not attaching too much importance to it. But we have to find the bastard and nail him down. I'll have a word with IG Police too."

October 4th

It had been *a long night as a security guard. One of the guards was absent and he had to cover for him too. But he had at least two hours before Sara woke up.*

It was time to reassess the events in Delhi and learn from the mistakes. Looking around the room, his gaze locked on the mat below the altar. The strand of hair he had placed under one corner of the mat was in the same position.

Picking up a thin nylon rope with a wire at one end, kept in the corner of the room, he pushed aside the well-worn jute mat. The four two by two feet tiles below lay there undisturbed. Each of the tiles had two rough holes. He threaded the wire into one hole and pulled from the other, looping the rope in the two holes in the tile. Pulling up the ends of the rope he lifted the tiles one by one, revealing crude steps disappearing below. He kept the tiles on the mat, taking care not to make any noise.

Taking out a torch from his backpack, he went down the narrow stairs that broadened as he descended into the small basement. It had been an arduous task to build the basement without raising the neighbors' suspicion. He had dug up the two rooms that ran below his and Sara's rooms after buying the house. The whole exercise took him one full year to get the entire setup as he wanted.

One room served as the vault for his arms and surveillance, and the other for his meditation and worship. At the end of the stairs, he lit a gas lamp and stood admiring his prized possessions—the guns and various arms collected over the years—in one of the open cupboards.

This was also a place from where he could see the world.

He switched on the various monitors aligned on one of the walls. One by one, the front and rear sides of Seth's family houses, and offices came alive. The footage was being recorded even in his absence using the portable battery-operated system he had indigenously installed, with enough backup for three days. He had been able to install the cameras on the buildings that overlooked the Seth properties, so he only knew the comings and goings. But he had full coverage on the Jindal family.

Unzipping the backpack, he took out his day's shopping— parts of the sniper he was going to assemble for his next rendezvous with Mr. Vikramaditya Seth, an electronic part which one of the monitors required, and a couple of hard disks.

It was now time to contemplate the past and think about the next steps.

Taking off his clothes, he cleaned himself the best he could from the water in the pitcher kept in the corner, wrapped a clean saffron dhoti around his legs and loins, and looped the sacred thread, the janeyu, on his shoulder across his chest. Taking a deep breath, he entered the dark, inner room, his spiritual sanctum.

'Om Krim Kaaliaaye Namah...'

In the shadow of the gas lamp behind him, the eyes of the life-sized deity, carved on one of the walls, followed him as he crossed the room and sat on a mat in front of the deity. Maa was angry.

Asking for forgiveness, for he had failed her again, he lit the incense and the sacred brass lamp at her feet. The room came alive with the fragrance under the warm glow of the yellow flame. The yellow light also revealed the pattern painted on the platform right in the center that matched with the one on his right upper arm. It was composed of a central point within five inverted triangles, three circles, and eight petals inside and outside. The whole drawing was then enclosed in a square with four closed doors.

He sat in the lotus position and picked up the knife kept near the platform. Heating the knife in the flame for a few seconds, he pricked at the center of the pattern on his arm with the pointed edge. Blood spurted from the cut. He held his arm over the pattern on the platform. Two drops of blood fell right in the middle. He then placed the knife back and picked up the string with the 108-rudraksh beads. Closing his eyes, he sat back with his forefinger and thumb joined, his hands resting on his knees. Trying to clear his mind from the chatter of failure, he began reciting the mantra to appease the deity 'Om Krim Kaaliaaye Namah'.

He concentrated on the position of the third eye on his forehead, the point between his eyebrows, and chanted the words counting on the holy beads on the rudraksh string. Today, he pictured a candle burning right at the center of his inner vision. A long, thick, white wax candle with an ivory silk wick at the center, burned with a bluish-amber petal shaped flame. The black clouds of chaos receded slowly in the warm glow of the candle, guiding him through the dark path that was his life.

Too many people around the target, someone had fallen at the same time he had pulled the trigger. Baggah had stood up. The candle flickered with the blasts of his meandering thoughts. He brought his concentration back on the orange-

red flame and the thin blue color around the wick of the candle. The flame steadied.

The years of training and preparation had gone waste because of one implausible odd. He would have to start from scratch again. The money would have to be arranged, a venue would have to be researched. Had he fired too early? He loved the Magnum that was customized to his specifications and felt bad that he had to leave it behind. Thinking about the attachments and affections, which he tried to minimize, made the flame flicker dangerously. He concentrated. The flare struggled for life, then finally snuffed out, leaving a thin line of grey smoke drifting up on the dark canvas of his mind. He sighed and tried to reignite the warm flare, but nothing happened.

⸺⊰⊱⸺

METRO TRAIN, NEW DELHI
4TH OCTOBER, 9:00 PM

The creep slipped his hand between the two girls again and felt the waist of the one on the right. The girl squirmed and moved her elbow closer to her body. The man straightened in the crowded compartment of the metro, looking in the opposite direction. Esha's jaw clenched, again, and she took a deep breath to relax. She was as angry at the girl for silently suffering the leech, as she was with the scum for taking advantage of the teenager.

As the crowd moved out at the next station, the girl took a few steps away from the man, but the man also moved with the girl. Esha couldn't stand the mixture of fear, helplessness, and embarrassment on the girl's face.

As some more of the crowd moved out at the next station, the girl hefted her backpack on her shoulder and turned to throw a hateful look towards the lecher. To Esha's surprise, the man grinned and winked at the girl, who tightened her lips and fixed her gaze on the darkened window. Without the advantage of the packed crowd, the man stayed away from the girl.

Realizing that the worst was over, Esha glanced outside the window, but there was nothing to see except their reflections. It was dark outside. The next stop was Esha's destination. She glanced at the girl, who was also looking at her, fear apparent in her wide eyes. If Esha disembarked, the girl would be alone with the eve-teaser, who was busy nibbling his nails as he studied both of them one by one. He took out his cell phone and spoke to someone in a low voice. Was he calling someone else? Esha's conscience didn't allow her to leave the girl alone.

The train slowed as her station approached. Esha stood rooted to her spot as the train doors slid shut. She decided she would take an auto back.

As the train stopped at the last station, Esha gestured to the girl to walk ahead of her. The man grimaced and rolled his eyes. The platform was long and deserted. If a police guard was posted, there was no sign of him. Esha walked behind the girl.

Another man, in his forties, appeared on the steps going down for the exit, barring their way. The man from the train caught hold of the girl's hand and growled, "Come with me, quietly."

"No…" she whispered, struggling against the grip.

"Leave her," Esha said, loosening her limbs.

"Stay out of this..." The older man by the stairs said, his eyes on the girl.

"I said leave her hand." Esha's tone made the men turn. With a slight, menacing smile, the older one gave her a once over with a lingering lecherous glance at her breasts.

"Hey Shanky, this one wants to get laid too."

"Let the girl go." Esha came onto her toes.

"Or what..." The older man took a step closer to her but stopped when another voice growled from behind.

"What's happening here?"

Esha sighed and glanced at Nikhil Mahajan leaning against the nearest platform pillar, watching the whole drama. He straightened and walked towards them to stand beside Esha. Shanky left the girl's arm, who ran and positioned herself behind Esha. She was trembling but otherwise composed.

"What took you so long?" Esha asked.

Mahajan's eyes widened at her unsurprised response. Grinning, he touched two fingers to his temple. "I'm impressed, Major."

"And who are you?" The older man now stepped back with Shanky falling in line with him, the street belligerence absent in their posture.

Flexing his wrist, Mahajan ignored them and glanced at Esha and the girl. "Shall we go, sweethearts?"

Esha nodded. The duo made no attempt to follow them.

⟩⟨⟩⟨⟩⟨⟩

A CAFE, NEW DELHI
4TH OCTOBER, 10:30 PM

"When did you notice me at the station? I must be losing my touch!" After dropping the girl home with some strict instructions on safety, they were sitting in a café, at Mahajan's insistence.

"On the train, and no, you are not. Losing your touch, I mean. I had sensed your presence the moment I entered the train and then saw you. I have that knack. Moreover, your height makes it hard for you to blend in with the crowd."

"Aah... my traitorous height."

"Were you following me?"

"No. Your ex-boss told me about your farewell party from the army today and that you will be at the metro station around eight p.m. By the time I located you, you were getting into the train, two compartments away from where I was. I didn't have a choice but to board the train. But I didn't feel like wading through the ocean of breathing, sweating, talking humanity, so stayed back."

Esha nodded.

"You shouldn't take risks like you did today. What if there were more men at the station?"

"Can't help it." She shrugged.

"Hmm... on to the business at hand then." He began once the waiter had served them and left. He kept a file on the table upside down, which she was sure had her name on it. "I know you have completed your SSC tenure in the army and are at a loose end. I want to hire you."

She smiled. "What's the nature of work?"

"This is not a regular security assignment, Major Sinha. I want your consent signed and documented, and only then can I disclose the details."

"Nothing illegal I hope."

He chuckled shaking his head. "It's an undercover bodyguard job in Mumbai, though the demand on your time might be more than what you would have bargained for and comes with risks."

"What's the tenure?"

"Two months... at a maximum, three."

"And after that?"

He shrugged. "As of now, this is what I can offer."

Then he quoted the remuneration and Esha's heart whistled. The sum could keep the family happy for at least two years and would pay for her sister Nisha's wedding in three months.

"Let me think about it."

"I'm afraid I don't have much time, Major."

"You'll have my answer by tomorrow, eight a.m." She stood up and held out her hand.

⸺⸺◈⸺⸺

October 5th

The insistent ringing of the phone jolted Esha out of deep slumber. She thought it was her alarm and jabbed on the side table but couldn't find the alarm clock. The ringing stopped but started again. She opened one eye. A faint glow from her cell phone indicated an incoming call.

Closing her eyes, Esha picked up her phone and put it to her ear.

"Esha? Major? Sorry to disturb you, sweetheart... I won't be available tomorrow. Esha, are you there?"

"Yes, Mr. Mahajan."

"Call me Nick, everyone does. I won't be in Mumbai tomorrow, I've briefed Maria about you. Reach the corporate office and ask for Maria at Vikram's office. She will know what to do. Don't say anything to anyone, except that you have been recruited in Maria's place. I'll be back by afternoon and will handle your joining formalities. Thanks."

"But... Mr. Mahajan... Nikhil..." After two seconds, she realized the call was disconnected. She frowned. The guy for sure moved fast. She had accepted the assignment in the morning and all official papers—the appointment letter, confidentiality agreement, and her ticket to Mumbai—had been delivered at her home by evening.

What a man! And people were not allowed to call her 'sweetheart', especially someone whom she would be reporting to. He would be her boss, how could he call her 'sweetheart'? She would set him right at the first opportunity, she vowed and tried to burrow in the pillow wishing for a few hours of uninterrupted sleep.

October 6th

Monday morning, Esha stood in front of the imposing twenty-one floor building that housed the corporate office of Seth Industries, one of the landmarks of Nariman Point, Mumbai. Looking at her reflection in the glass-cladded façade, she grimaced at her formal trouser-suit. The jacket was necessary for hiding the shoulder holster. She sweated like a pig in the sultry weather, despite the antiperspirant she had liberally sprayed all over herself.

Taking a deep breath, she walked through the revolving door and stood there staring. The triple height air-conditioned lobby, clad in white and grey Italian marble, had a contemporary white sculpture that was shapeless yet stylish. A huge ball-like chandelier hung above the sculpture, beyond which nestled the chrome and marble reception area. A huge mural depicting the logo of Seth Industries adorned the wall behind the reception desk.

On the right, black leather sofas were kept for visitors along with a kiosk for water and a coffee machine. The entry to the office was to the left, beyond the security barricades. She could see two elevators and a door, which she guessed must be to access the stairs.

Manning the reception desk was the Indian versions of Barbie and Ken, with western clothes but black hair. Esha tried not to look amused as she approached the reception desk. The girl looked up.

"Esha Sinha, I'd like to meet Maria, at Mr. Seth's office."

A pair of heavily kohled eyes and mascara thickened lashes assessed her from head to toe and asked, "This is regarding?"

"I'm joining the office today, in place of Maria."

Barbie exchanged a look with Ken. "Do you have an appointment?"

"Yes, I believe so." A neatly arched eyebrow went up. "Yes, I have one." Esha amended quickly.

The epitome of style and fashion sighed and dialed a number on the board. "There is a Miss... what did you say your name was?" She tilted her chin forward.

"Esha Sinha."

"Yes... Esha Sinha for Maria." She giggled. "Says, she is coming in Maria's place." Another giggle. "Okay."

It seemed there was another bitch at the other end since Barbie glanced at Esha and giggled again. Esha narrowed her glance.

"I'm sorry Miss..." She tried to contain her glee behind a polite facade. "You are not on our appointment list. We are not hiring."

"If you contact her, she'll tell you that I'm expected." Esha clenched her teeth.

"I'm sorry, but that's not the protocol. We are not supposed to call Mr. Seth's office without an appointment." She exchanged another raised eyebrows look with Ken and he shook his head. The painted Barbie dismissed Esha like a fungus inflected blusher and went to work on her monitor.

Esha felt like flashing her identity and bashing their perfectly bleached denture in. Furious with Nikhil Mahajan and everyone associated with him, she called up his number, but there was no response. What the hell? The least he could have done was leave a message with the morons at the reception. She sat on the plush sofa kept alongside one wall and decided to wait for him.

After ten minutes, Ken nodded at the guard at the barricades and he marched to her. "Ma'am, you can't wait here without any reason."

"I have a valid reason, I'm waiting on Mr. Mahajan's instructions. I have to meet Maria."

"She is not in the office. I'm sorry Miss, we can't allow you to sit here."

«Fine, I'm going.»

Esha looked around and went towards the kiosk behind the potted fern. Weighing her options, she took a glass of water from the dispenser and studied the barricaded entry to the elevators. The barricades were waist high and operated with the help of a magnetic card issued for visitors by the security.

A couple of employees came in through the outer doors. A fat lady ambled outside the glass doors, rummaging in one of her two large purses, a laptop bag dangling from one shoulder. Taking the decision to nick the lady's I-card, Esha marched towards the exit door and banged into someone.

"Steady..." Someone with a familiar voice held her with an accustomed light touch on her shoulder, and that same whiff of expensive tobacco assailed her nose.

Esha glanced up to find Vikram Seth smiling at her.

«Oh, I... I'm sorry.»

"We meet again, Maj... er... Ms. Sinha." He let go of her and extended his hand.

She had no choice but to place hers in his, a tingle running down her toes. Her hand was subjected to a firm shake that she returned, masking her bizarre reaction to him.

"Why am I having... kind of a... *déjà vu* moment?" His smile stretched to show a perfect set of white teeth.

The wind ruffled Vikram's hair and Esha's heart somersaulted. When did he become Vikram for her? She pursed her lips to rein in her jumping hormone levels.

"Sir, I think we should go inside." A man in a black suit interrupted.

"Yes, of course." Vikram moved forward to hold the door open and ushered her inside with a hand on her elbow. "Jay, meet Ms. Sinha. She is joining in place of Maria."

Esha would never forget the look on the faces of Barbie and Ken as she entered the lobby again. Vikram took her to the security barricade and instructed the guards to issue a temporary card for her and escort her to his office.

To her surprise, it was Barbie who escorted her to his office. The girl kept glancing at her, from time to time, probably wondering about the swift appointment and dying of curiosity. Apparently, Maria was on leave.

Esha studied the surroundings as the elevator lobby opened into a glass-encased office that had two desks and a plush sofa for guests or other employees to wait. Barbie number two sat at one of the desks, while the other one was vacant. The heavily made-up girl looked up from the computer and raised her fine eyebrows.

Aware of the exchange of glances and the passing of silent messages between the two, Esha scanned and memorized the layout and the exit. Beyond the assistants' area, she could see an ornate wood-paneled door, which she guessed would lead to the den of the high and mighty Mr. Vikramaditya Seth, Jr.

Barbie number two spoke with someone over the phone and said, "Ms. Sinha, you may go inside." She waved her hand towards the heavy teak door.

Pushing the door open, Esha entered and stopped short at the view.

Spread before her was the wide expanse of what one would call the heart of Mumbai. She moved forward on automaton, forgetting the two men in the room. The entire front wall was made of glass, from one end to the other, from the floor to the eleven feet high ceiling, showing the full landscape of Nariman Point and its surrounding areas. It seemed the city was at their feet, running under them. The world beneath was a playground with toy vehicles and Lilliputians going about their businesses. And whosoever was in this very room was the king, the ruler.

After a couple of stunned moments, her ears registered the muted hum of conversation and she forced herself to pay attention to the proceedings in the room. She reluctantly brought her gaze from the glass wall to the desk to her right and noticed Vikram watching her as if he understood and shared her dazed awe.

That moment, a deep, unknown bond connected them. Her reaction to him at the Golf Club seemed like a mild breeze that could only ruffle feathers, compared to the way she responded to him in that instant.

The older man, studying a file, called out to him and those mid-night black eyes turned to the papers spread over the table. The moment passed. She exhaled and glanced at the wall again, but the view had lost its charm to the man at the desk.

What's with this guy? She had met all kinds of virile, intelligent men and dealt with them with her legendary indifference. But, what's with this guy? She frowned. Why did her heart always react like a teenager's when he was around? She wasn't sure of the answer.

Making her face blank, she returned her attention to the room or rather him sitting behind the huge teak table. He was on the phone now, leaning back in his chair, slowly swiveling it in an arc. The scar on his cheek appeared more pronounced as the bright morning sunlight fell on his face. How did he get that big a scar? He could have gotten plastic surgery done but the fact that he hadn't spoke volumes about his character.

To her surprise, she spied another, similar scar on his right forearm, running below the elbow and disappearing under the strap of his wristwatch. The smoke assaulted her almost immediately as she noticed the cigarette in his hand. She turned away again and discreetly tried to breathe through her mouth. Mumbai below went about its business, indifferent to the turbulence in her mind.

"Ms. Sinha." Vikram stood beside her.

The older man had left.

"I'm sorry." She stood to attention.

"No problem. The view has that effect on most of the people who enter the room for the first time. I'm rather proud of it and would have been disappointed if you were not impressed by my window to the outside world."

She fought the urge to look at him when he stood savoring the scene outside in silence, watching the city going about its business—fast and with purpose.

"Am I assigned to your security, Mr. Seth?" Esha finally asked.

"Yes."

Goddamn! Her stomach churned at the confirmation of something she had been dreading all along. She had hoped she would be assigned to either his mother or sister when Nikhil had mentioned the assignment. Hiding her panic behind a nod, she asked, "Is this glass bullet-proof?"

He glanced at her, laughter lurking in his eyes just like on that day at the hotel in Delhi. It took all her energy and focus to keep her face impassive, but she couldn't control the sarcasm from creeping into her voice. "Something funny?"

"I'm wondering, how a person at five feet eight could be a bodyguard for someone who is six feet and wider than her."

The fact that he didn't mention her gender brought mild relief to her peeve. "The protection needn't be only physical. One needs wit and agility to tackle tight situations."

He nodded. "Agreed. That's the reason I've never questioned Nick's wisdom in these matters. Why were you rushing outside?"

"I wasn't."

"It didn't seem like that in the lobby."

"Your staff refused to let me in, so I was trying another way."

"Is there another way?" He frowned. "I'm intrigued."

"I was trying to nick the lady's I-card, the one who was on your right."

"You could have?"

"Yes."

"What if you were caught?"

"I wouldn't have been."

"That's some confidence."

"Is the glass bulletproof?" She changed the subject.

He chuckled and said, "Yes."

"Can anyone access it from the roof?" She looked up but couldn't see anything beyond the parapet roof.

"I don't think so, though I've never given it a thought since we are on the twenty-first floor. Nick may have some information on it."

"How many exits are there in this room?"

"Two." Glancing at his watch, Vikram sighed and raked his fingers through his hair. "No matter how much I want this discussion to continue, I can't. There's a meeting in two minutes."

"I'll speak to Mr. Mahajan."

"You will work as my PA in place of Maria, who is going on maternity leave. Nick will brief you on the details when he comes back around lunch."

Nervousness crept on her again at the thought of working closely with Vikram, for most of the twenty-four hours in a day.

"Don't worry, I'll guide you," he added.

The panic increased double-fold. She didn't want to be guided by him.

"Koel, my other PA, will also be there. Though according to Nick's grand scheme of things, no one should know about this except the three of us."

She hadn't realized she had become so transparent, but he mistook the panic on her face as someone dreading the responsibilities of a PA. That was some saving grace. She nodded at the appropriate pauses in the conversation.

"Why don't you sit with Koel and go through the company brochures?" All business, he pressed the intercom. "Koel, please come..."

Barbie number two, from the desk outside, opened the door and walked in. Esha rubbed her nose.

"Koel, this is Ms. Esha Sinha, Maria's temporary replacement. Between her and you, I think we will manage in Maria's absence. Ms. Sinha doesn't have much experience, so go easy and help her as required."

Esha was sure Koel hid a smirk behind a fake cough she had suddenly developed.

⊷⊶

Esha sneezed the moment she closed Vikram's office door behind her. Three in succession.

"Wha...at happened to you?" Koel scowled.

"I'm allergic."

"To Vikram?" She smirked openly this time "You better be," she added.

"To cigarette smoke." Esha corrected with a fleeting indifferent glance. The look worked on most of the haughty women and it did on Koel too, who huffed and sat on her seat.

Esha passed her time reading the brochures and the boring annual reports of Seth Industries for all of two hours. A headache brewed at her temples. She looked at her watch—it was two p.m.—and her stomach growled, empty after the breakfast she had had during the flight and the two cups of coffee thereafter.

Just then, the elevator pinged. Esha looked up to see Nikhil enter the office, shaking his head, grinning. She stood up and sighed. He exuded so much warmth that there was no way she could be angry or formal with him.

"Oh, I'm so sorry darling, never realized that Maria will call in sick." He took Esha by her arm and steered her towards the lift. "Koel dear, I need to do security checks and brief Ms. Sinha today, so she'll start work tomorrow. Will Maria be in the office tomorrow?"

"Yeah... that's what she had told me." Koel sat on her desk, dismissing them without a second glance. Her response to him was surprising. She was as immune to Nikhil's charm as he was oblivious of his good looks.

Nikhil escorted Esha to a small conference room outside Vikram's office area.

"Have a seat."

"I prefer standing when I take orders."

"Esha, sweetheart, forget that you are in the army. You'll blow your cover behaving like this. Just relax. Sit."

She pulled a chair. "I request you to address me by my name. I'm not used to my superiors calling me 'sweetheart'." Though she didn't give in to the urge to pout, she was agitated and a little disturbed that she couldn't control her distress at the informal way he addressed her.

"It is to loosen you a bit to us civilians, and for God's sake, I'm not your boss." Nikhil continued quickly when he noticed her squirming in the chair. "Yes, you will report to me. But for appearances' sake, Vikram is your boss. You are his PA, so behave like one."

"Yeah sure, but I can't behave like that girl and I can't wear skirts. They aren't practical and I hate putting anything on my face—the smell makes me sneeze."

Throwing his head back, Nikhil laughed and shook his head. "You know, I have a complete six-inch dossier on you and I'm yet to come across any info that you are remotely thick-headed. Are you putting up an act? Or, is it something else? Wait a minute! Are you nervous? What are you nervous of?"

"No... I'm not nervous. Please continue."

He sat back and crossed his arms. "You are nervous. Does Vikram make you nervous?"

"No, not at all," she said in a breathless, quick reply.

Nikhil leaned in, his eyebrows furrowing. "Don't be. He is the quietest, most undemanding guy. I'm the ogre. At least, that's what my team tells me." He patted her hand and smiled. "Tell me about the French embassy episode. Was that the last time you shot someone?"

Now her eyebrows went up. "How do you know about that? It was supposed to be confidential. The newspapers there were banned from reporting about the incident."

"Calm down, Xena. I have my sources." Nikhil smiled and ignored her scowl at the nickname. "Moreover, I'm not going to report it to the media. I wanted to know whether you've fired a gun in real circumstances. As you very well know, shooting during the training and the guts required in real life are a different matter altogether."

She nodded and said, "In Paris, as you must have seen in the report, the Ambassadress' daughter was planning to elope with this French guy who was a drug addict. Ma'am ordered me to follow him and generally keep a track on his activities. One night he tried to sneak in into the embassy, and I had to shoot him in the leg when he refused to stand still even after my repeated warnings. It was one hell of a night."

Nikhil smiled and opened another file. "Coming to the problem at hand, Vikram has a terrorist threat from outside the country. And he does not want Z-security around him. We are still investigating the incident." Gone was the frivolous person he portrayed to the world at large, Esha noted, as he briefed her about her responsibilities. His face had taken a hard, determined edge. "From this day onwards, either you, or I, or both of us, have to stick with him like glue."

"Terrorists normally blow everyone to eliminate their target."

"That's right. My team sanitizes his vehicles and the public locations before he goes any place. We rely heavily on electronic surveillance. You'll be staying on the premises, the first floor of the outhouse, where I live on the ground floor. Apart from the two of us, the only person who lives in-house is his butler-cum-chef Kishore *dada*. All the other servants come and go and are checked thoroughly by the guards posted at the gate."

Esha nodded, as Nikhil explained the security net around Vikram Seth. She had to admit she was quite impressed with his strategy.

"I want you to come early in the morning and make sure everything is sanitized. I'll escort him to the office in the morning. You will stay with him throughout the day, wherever he goes, and escort him back in the night. I have replaced his regular driver with Jay, my associate, whom I trust with my eyes closed, but even he doesn't have the complete picture. Apart from the three of us, another armored vehicle follows his car with four more guards."

He briefed her about the security arrangements that he had made for Vikram's office as well as for his two residences in Mumbai. He took care of the security arrangements for Vikram's mother as well, who lived in one of their apartment buildings in Hiranandani, in the Powai neighborhood in Mumbai. They discussed the nuances of the security in Vikram's cars, the jet, and the helicopter. He showed her the security room used for monitoring the CCTV cameras.

"These are your papers, complete with an MBA degree. And here is the gun you prefer and the license to go with it." Nikhil handed her the file and the gun.

"Any motive behind the attack?"

"We have some theory, but things aren't adding up."

"Who are the beneficiaries?"

"His mother and sister."

"What about Viraj Seth?"

"Why do you think it is not the terrorists?"

"You know... explore all the angles and stuff."

"Yes, I agree."

"Any progress on the investigations in Delhi?"

"Police are pursuing all the leads." Nikhil opened her file again.

Esha had an inkling he didn't want to talk about it, either because they were in the office or because he didn't trust her enough. It was fair, she concluded, given the seriousness of the matter, so she dropped the subject.

Nikhil looked up and smiled. "Though you are not required to wear makeup, please be at ease and behave less like an army Major."

She couldn't help but flash an answering smile. "As long as I'm not required to paint my face."

"You're not. The gun in its case will not show in the security checks in this office and at home. But elsewhere, be a little careful, make up some story."

"No problem." Esha checked the gun and loaded the magazine, happy to have something familiar in the new surroundings.

"Where's your luggage?" He asked her, as they returned to the conference room. She told him about the cloakroom at the airport. He called up someone and arranged for it to be brought to Vikram's house. "How about dinner tonight?"

Confused, she frowned. "Are we allowed to have dinner out?"

"Not for a few months. But if he is eating out then we can, at the same restaurant. And I have asked him to not go out unless it is unavoidable." He winked, back to his Casanova avatar, turning on the full charm of his killer smile. "How about dinner at my place? The time saved in commuting could be put to better use."

She chuckled at the transformation. "I don't go out with my superiors."

"But your boss is Vikram, Xena."

Esha chuckled as she shook her head.

SETH TOWERS, MUMBAI
6TH OCTOBER, 5:00 PM

Vikram couldn't concentrate on the budget spreadsheet on the screen. His thoughts kept going to his new PA-cum-bodyguard. She was a class apart—

restrained and understated but elegantly so. And then there was that lisp, totally in contrast to her serious demeanor, kind of endearing.

The morning hadn't started well for her, and then there was Mumbai from his office. Her eyes, otherwise shuttered, couldn't hide her reaction to the view. She had experienced the same heady power as he had when he had first walked into the room years ago. The view from the glass wall had that effect on people, and the fact that she was mesmerized by it, invoked a kind of pride in him. Vikram narrowed his eyes. Why would he want her to be impressed by anything he had? He had stopped impressing people a long time back.

Today, she was a little flustered in his office, but recovered fast, presenting the professional mask she always wore. He wondered what he would find if the mask was removed. He knew she took her job seriously—she was deeply offended when he had brushed off her inferences on the shooting that day in Delhi. Today also, she had disliked his casual reference to her being a bodyguard. He also knew she was engaged once, to her colleague. He wondered what had gone wrong.

Vikram took out the file on Esha Sinha. No. Major Esha Sinha. Though Nikhil had briefed him about her history, he had left the file for his perusal. He chuckled and shook his head as he read the title on her file—Nikhil and his humor.

Eroica

(E-Major)

Beethoven - Third Symphony

"The office closes at six pm," Koel informed Esha, collecting her things from the desk. "We have instructions from Vikram sir to leave the office at closing time. He often works late and gets furious if anyone stays beyond the office hours."

"Thanks…" Esha replied when Koel kept standing at her desk.

"Trying to impress the boss?" Koel said, trying to peer at the screen, which Esha had flicked off. "You don't have a chance with Vikram. Stick with Nick, you might get a piece of the pie. The likes of you are employed as his maids or are good only for a night's association."

"Have a grand night, Koel."

Koel whirled around and left the room.

Esha sighed and resumed browsing the Internet.

It was ten minutes to nine and there was no sign of any movement from Vikram's office. She had eaten nothing since breakfast, surviving on the coffee from the vending machine. Her innards churned, demanding sustenance, but leaving her desk was not an option. She searched in her bag and found a nutri-bar. She hated them but unwrapped it.

As she ate, she stretched her arms up to get the blood circulation going into her aching muscles and, right then, the door opened. Startled, she stood up and her cell phone slipped to the floor. She bent down to pick it up and banged her head against the table corner and cursed under her breath. Standing up, she discreetly crumpled the nutri-bar wrapper in her fist, hoping he didn't hear the crunching sound it made.

"Oh… I forgot that you were waiting. Did you hurt yourself?" He had been working for straight seven hours after lunch and looked tired.

She shook her head and hooked the Bluetooth to her ear. "Ready to go? Land or air?"

"I've asked Jay to bring the car around."

Esha nodded and they both entered the lift. As the lift doors closed shut, she went still. The feeling she had experienced in his office intensified in the closed, confined space with him. They stood facing the door, he a step behind her. Sensing his eyes on her, she focused her mind on the descending numbers on the front panel.

The lift stopped at the eleventh floor. She glanced back at him, gun in her hand.

"My mother's office. But no one should be there at this hour."

She gestured to him to stand in the recessed corner beside the door. To her relief, he moved into the corner without any question as she stepped into the opposite corner. The lift doors swished open. She flicked off the safety catch on the gun. Nobody entered. The doors slid close. She exhaled and slipped the gun back into the holster.

"Who could have done that?" Esha frowned, talking to herself.

Vikram shrugged. The question didn't warrant an answer.

The lift doors opened on the ground floor. The limousine, chauffeured by Jay, waited at the porch. She hurried to open the vehicle door for him before Jay could get out. But Vikram took the door handle from her and motioned her to sit first. She didn't protest since she didn't want him exposed in the open for too long, but anger started simmering. He slipped in next to her and closed the door.

She turned towards him, eyes flashing, ready to set a few ground rules. Before she could open her mouth, his phone rang. Throughout the drive, he was busy over his phone discussing something about equity, mutual funds, and market trends. As they reached home, he went inside the bungalow without a backward glance, the cell still glued to his ear. She decided to broach the subject in the morning.

Esha's luggage stood outside the outhouse. The guard at the gate handed her the keys to the first-floor studio apartment. It was a neat two-floor building and the apartment was quite a luxury, considering she was a mere employee. The room had a recessed kitchenette to the right of the entrance and a couch to the left. Beyond the kitchen was the small door to the washroom and the bed was on left. An easy chair and a coffee table completed the room's setup.

The kitchenette had everything needed to cook an adequate meal for two. The three-door French windows on the front wall, next to the bed, opened into a tiny balcony, with a view of the high boundary wall laden with purple-pink bougainvillea. No one could see inside or outside, which was good, she thought. There was another smaller window above the couch, which opened to reveal the main bungalow's entrance. Everything had an unused feel to it as if refurbished only recently.

Esha liked it. It was bigger and better than the room she had shared with Nisha back home.

She was half-way through unpacking when a car drove into the driveway. She peered through the white lace curtains of the smaller window. A Mercedes stopped at the entrance to the portico and a lady dressed in a short black dress rushed up the steps. She recognized Karisma, Vikram's current girlfriend, a lawyer, from the dossier Nikhil had given her on all the people and vehicles that had access to the premises.

No matter how hard she tried, Esha couldn't pry herself away from the window. But when her stomach growled, she had to bring her attention back to her basic needs. She had a pack of biscuits stashed somewhere and delved into her bag, searching for it. After five minutes, someone screamed and a door slammed shut. She hurried to the window and saw the woman storm down the porch steps, get into the car and drive away with the tires screeching.

An unidentified calm settled in her heart, surprising her. Why was she so happy that his girlfriend didn't stay? Why was she behaving so irrationally? He was an assignment for two months, a monetary transaction. After that, they would go back to their separate worlds and in their own ways, never to meet again. This had to stop.

Placing her palms over her eyes, she focused on her responsibilities, and remembered Samar, his parents, her father, and her family. She relived the humiliation, the pain, and lamented on the would-have-beens. She recalled her shattered dreams and her vow to never dream again. Vikram Seth was an assignment, a financial ticket to Nisha's wedding and her family's economic security.

Someone knocked on her door. She opened it to see an elderly, white-haired man standing outside with a tray in his hands.

"Dinner," the man said, when she stared at him. "*Baba's* orders." He was a man of few words, Esha realized. She liked him already and took the tray.

So, he had noticed the nutri-bar.

❦

SUBURBS, MUMBAI
6TH OCTOBER, 11:30 PM

The phone rang *for two seconds, then stopped. He looked at the display and opened a drawer. Selecting a SIM card from this collection of fifteen-odd cards from varied service providers, he opened the back panel of the mobile. He replaced the original, then dialed the caller. The call was picked up immediately.*

"Mahajan has replaced Seth's driver with Jay, the tall fellow with a mole. They must have hired a private investigator too, I'm on it."

"Hmm..."

"Don't wait too much. They think that the attack was by the Burmese rebels. Any attack within the next two-three weeks will also be attributed to the terrorists."

"I can't. I need to be prepared."

"You have to do something fast!"

"Don't pressure me. Do you want me to die or worse, get caught?" He had never liked it when someone pushed him.

"Of course not!"

The concern for him was back and he exhaled. "Don't worry. Leave everything to me."

"Can't we hire someone else?"

"And include one more breathing entity into the secret? Have you gone mad?"

"These things can be done anonymously too."

He remained silent. The call was disconnected.

He turned to find Sara standing with that pretty, old doll cradled in her arms. The lever on the cupboard had come loose and she had been able to open the door from her side. He made a mental note to fix it.

"How are you?" he asked, masking his grief at the picture she made in the clean yet tattered clothes, her thinning, ginger hair curled around her face in the style she wore thirty years back.

"Please bring milk, Anna is hungry." She had begun rocking the doll as she turned to go back.

Sighing, he sat down and took off his shoes. She would forget her demand the moment she saw the other toys in her room.

October 7th

Moving towards the balcony of his bedroom, Vikram lit a cigarette and took in the sight. Major Esha Sinha, in a navy-blue track pant and a sleeveless white tee, jogged on the paved path around the bungalow. His eyes followed her rhythmic, energetic run until she disappeared from his sight around the corner.

As he savored his morning nicotine fix, he watched her take round after round, increasing the speed with each, and lasting a shorter duration in front of his eyes. With the Bluetooth receiver in her ear and eyes down, she wasn't aware of his presence on the balcony.

He had gone through her complete dossier and was impressed. Apart from the rarity that being a woman she was part of the NSG, Esha had excelled in all kinds of training there, sometimes even outshining her male counterparts. The only shadow was her broken engagement—the reason listed was incompatibility and she had put an end to the relationship, which didn't ring true. She didn't seem like someone who'd go back on her decision. Or maybe, Vikram wondered, he had read her wrong.

When she didn't appear for the next round, he became curious and went to the family room in front of the house. Was the exercise over? Must be, she had been running for more than half an hour without breaking any sweat.

He peered through the curtains from the first-floor living area and saw her doing push-ups on the ground in front of the outhouse. His cigarette forgotten between his fingers, he enjoyed her profile and neat moves in the power exercises she did. He hadn't known that watching a woman exercise would be so appealing. It had been a treat to watch her in the lift too, completely at ease with the gun. Nikhil had chosen well.

Esha ran and caught hold of a branch of the tree in the compound and pulled herself fifteen times with her legs close to her body. Incredible, Vikram thought. The branch swung down, making it difficult for her to pull up, but she did it.

Nikhil had come out of his room and stood watching her complete the workout. He said something to her when she finished and she laughed aloud, a merry infectious sound, and Vikram found himself smiling. A moment later she punched Nikhil's shoulder playfully and they went to their rooms. He wondered at the easy repartee shared by the two.

He took the last drag and went to the gym for his own morning fitness routine.

Vikram made it a habit to come to work one hour before everyone to plan his day in peace. He looked forward to the serene silence of the office in the morning hours and found it therapeutic to watch the city come alive from his office window.

But today, he wasn't the first person to step off the office lift. Esha sat at Koel's desk watching the monitor intently and at times typing on the keyboard furiously. Nikhil must have asked her to come early. Surprisingly, the intrusion didn't irritate him.

For an army person who had never held a desk job, Vikram noticed that she could type really fast. She had that latent energy around her that gave the impression that she could move in a microsecond if she wanted to.

Some may call her pretty, but she was definitely different. Today, she was wearing black trousers and a pale pink shirt. The light pink color was the only indication of her accepting her femininity—else she gave no sign of being conscious of the fact.

Her dusky face again had no makeup, and that looked a little odd to him, but she appeared fresh and cool. A lock of hair kept falling on her forehead, which she jerked in place with a slight movement of her head from time to time.

The moment Vikram realized she had sensed his presence, he moved forward, pretending to have just entered.

"Good morning." She stood straight in front of the desk with her hands behind the back, and head square to her shoulders—the smart army stance. She could have been a model with her height and lean figure. "Mr. Seth, may I have a word with you?"

Hiding his surprise at the request, he nodded and she followed him inside.

He kept his mobile on the desk, arranging the paperweight before he took out the Marlboro pack.

"It is of utmost importance that you don't expose yourself like you did when you opened the door for me last night." Lips pursed, she again stood in that straight posture.

"Agreed." She was genuinely agitated. He suppressed a smile. "Even I have something to say. You'll have to shed this crisp way you stand."

"Huh... I'm sorry." She quickly brought her hands to the front.

Her hands dangled at her sides, swinging a bit. She felt odd with him, most people did. Vikram smiled to bring her at ease. "You can hold a pen or your mobile and fiddle with it."

"Yeah... sure, thank you."

"Also, if you want everyone to believe that you are working as my PA you shouldn't behave like my bodyguard. And another thing to remember, none of my office employees open any door for me. I have forbidden it. I don't like people doing things for me that are not in their official 'terms of responsibilities'." He made quotation marks in the air.

She nodded. "I'll keep that in mind. Thank—"

"Where's your gun?" He didn't want her to leave.

"What...?"

"You were wearing a shoulder holster yesterday." He came forward and leaned against the corner of the table, striking the lighter against the cigarette pack. She took a step back.

"Oh, I have an ankle one today. May I le—"

"Vikram Seth..." Urvi's musical, yet angry voice rang out from the entrance.

Esha imperceptibly came to attention, then relaxed and turned towards the voice.

Vikram couldn't help but grimace at the interruption and sighed. "You surprise me, Urvi. I've never seen you up and painted so early in the morning." Urvi stood at the threshold with one hand on the door frame and the other on her waist, wearing an above-the-knee red skirt, a skimpy, frilly, white blouse, and silver stilettos.

"Why did you refuse to finance the film?" Urvi's shrill voice was in contrast to her glamorous entry. "Why did you cancel the project?" she shouted again when he lit his forgotten cigarette.

"It was a business decision."

"But, it was my re-launch project. I could kill you for this," she hissed.

Esha took one step towards her but stopped at the subtle movement of his head.

"I can't waste my money like that. I promised you a launch pad and you are foisting your brother on me as well. This won't do."

"What's wrong with his screenplay? And what authority do you have in this field?"

He narrowed his eyes and she stepped back. "Never question my authority or my decision, Urvi. You know you have never gotten far by doing that."

"Why, you basta—" Her hand went up in an arc and halted mid-way, caught in a vice-like grip before it could even reach anywhere near him.

Used to Urvi's tantrums, Vikram was already on guard, but the split-second action by Esha surprised even him. He hadn't noticed her move from her place.

Urvi's big eyes widened even more as she turned towards Esha. "How dare you, you bitch? Leave my hand."

She swung the other hand, which was also caught with no apparent effort.

"Vikram..." Urvi wailed.

Esha looked at him. Vikram nodded, and she released her hold.

"Look at what you've done, you... you bitch..., the marks will show now," Urvi screeched, rubbing her wrists. "Vikram darling, I want you to fire her at once." Her voice dripping with honey, she fluttered her eyelashes.

"Thank you, Esha. I'll call you later," he said.

"Who is she, your bodyguard or something? Vikram, you know I need the money and—"

<hr>

Esha couldn't help but hear the last sentence as she closed the door of his sanctum and exhaled. What a woman!

Her eyes darted towards the clock on her screen. It was eight twenty-two, she had been with him for only ten minutes but it felt like she had been tortured for ten hours straight. He stood so close, playing with the lighter, even as he advised her to relax. Goddamn!

She sat on the spare chair near Maria's desk, knowing Koel would not appreciate her nosing around her desk.

"Hi!"

She looked up to find a heavily pregnant woman entering. The sight of a pleasant, smiling person was a welcome relief to her after yesterday. She smiled and greeted her.

"Hi, I'm Maria. You must be Esha. I'm sorry, I couldn't come yesterday. Ready to start?" Maria said, firing up her PC. "Is Vikram in office?"

"Yes, and so is his wife." She recollected from the file Nikhil had provided.

"Wife? Oh, you mean Urvi. They are divorced. How come she is in so early? As far as I know, she never gets up before ten."

Esha shrugged. "She seems a little upset at something."

"Must be in need of money. They always want something or the other from him, always thinking of their own needs. Selfish all the way!" Maria shook her head and settled in her seat. "He never had time to even mourn his father properly. Bless his soul." Maria had worked with Seth Sr. for twelve years and was now working with Vikram.

The door to his office opened and Urvi stormed out muttering something, her blonde-streaked hair blowing behind her back.

"I don't understand. Why does he entertain her?" Maria shook her head.

"Good personal assistants do not gossip." Koel entered the office. With gorgeous hair and a petite personality, she could have been attractive if not for her permanent diva-like pout.

"Koel, did you finish that market research report I gave you yesterday?" Maria asked.

"What will be her responsibilities?" Koel ignored Maria's question to ask one of her own.

"She'll handle the appointments and will be with the boss for all meetings and conferences. The rest you will handle."

"I'm senior to her, so I should be doing what she has been assigned." Koel pouted even more.

"You are senior here, and you know the organization's history better than her, which is why you will handle the reports. Remember, in my absence, Vikram will look at all the reports directly. So be careful."

Her glances throwing daggers at Esha, Koel went to her desk. Esha, amused at the one-sided tug-of-words, looked at Maria with raised eyebrows.

"All of them want to be Mrs. Seth Jr.," Maria muttered.

The rest of the morning went by in a flurry of meetings, which Esha found hard to follow. What she came to realize later though was that documenting the minutes of the meeting was even harder.

Vikram stormed out ten minutes before lunch without his notebook, asking Maria to cancel his appointments for the next two hours.

⚜

VERSOVA, MUMBAI
7TH OCTOBER, 4:30 PM

Vikram brought the vehicle to a screeching halt right at the entrance lobby of Vandana's apartment building in Versova. He tossed the keys to Jay sitting beside him and ran out of the car.

Vandana's trusted housekeeper was standing by the entrance door as Vikram reached the twelfth floor.

"She is in the bathroom..." the woman said.

Vikram nodded and rushed inside. The two maids, talking in whispers in the living room, went silent at his thunderous gaze. He entered the bedroom and breathed in sharply.

After the elegantly ordered living room, the state of the bedroom came as a shock to Vikram. It was in utter disarray—the mattress was on the floor and the pillows lay ripped apart with the down-feathers dotting the carpet. The dressing table was devoid of all the bottles, tubes and knick-knacks that Vandana loved. They were scattered all over, some of them broken, staining the carpet, some rolling on the floor. *Daija*, Aaryan's nanny, was chanting something soothing, sitting on the floor beside the bathroom door with her holy string in her hand.

Taking a deep breath, Vikram knocked on the door. "*Di*... please open the door... everything will be all right."

When she whispered something from inside, he crouched down and pressed his ear to the keyhole. Unable to hear her words, he asked "Shall I call mamma? You know she'll worry and we shouldn't bother her, don't you think so?"

"Go away Vikram... nothing will help..." Vandana's voice was a mere whisper.

"She's upset," *daija* said. "I don't know who started the fight in the morning today..." She trembled and hiccupped, unable to finish the sentence.

Vikram patted her wrinkled hands. "It's okay *daija*, she will come out. Won't you *di*? Look, you are upsetting *daija*, she is so worried... please come out and we'll sort this out."

"He hit her again. She had a big bruise on her forehead in the morning... oh my baby." *Daija's* eyes filled and overflowed with tears. She wiped her tears with the *pallu* of her snowy-white, starched cotton sari.

Vikram pursed his lips at the picture she painted. This had happened intermittently over the years but nowadays it was frequent. He would have to find some closure for this. He knocked on the door again.

"Vandana *di*, why don't you come out and we can have a nice cup of tea and chat?"

Feet scuffled behind the door and it clicked open.

Vandana came out, clad in a pale blue silk negligee with a gown of a darker shade over it. His jaw clenched and his hands fisted. She was drenched in water waist down and the bruise on her left temple stood out like a beacon against the pale skin. Her lower lip was also bleeding on the left side.

He stepped forward and hugged her tight in his arms and she began crying again. He patted her back, rocked her, murmuring soothing words. All along, he kept thinking of ways to kill Jindal for torturing his sister like this.

Vandana stopped weeping after a few minutes and *daija* took over. She fawned over her with a towel, the maids were instructed to make ginger tea and tidy the bedroom. Vikram sat and waited in the living room.

He glanced up as she came out wearing a jumpsuit, her hair tamed into a ponytail. She looked so fragile and yet so beautiful.

"He is a bastard of the first order," Vandana said, her voice hoarse. "Gautam is having an affair."

"You know he won't have an affair. He is aiming for a seat in the parliament, he won't take that risk." Vikram rubbed her cold hands between his own. "Even the private investigators you had hired could not unearth anything."

"He is a chameleon Vikram, and I think he practices black-arts."

"Don't be silly! He is a public figure. How can he manage his company and political engagements and still find time to practice magic?"

"You don't know the powers of these things, he might have an alter ego—"

"Here is your breakfast and medicine, love." *Daija* came with a bottle, a maid wheeling the breakfast trolley behind her. "Look I have asked them to prepare everything you like."

Vandana hugged *daija* around the waist and tried to smile but winced. "What will I do without you!"

Vandana sighed and wiped a lone tear. "It's of no use Vikram, he will always deny it. He never loses control in front of anyone. Ask *daija*. The shouting and insulting, everything happens when we are alone. He is trying to portray me as a mental case so that he can get rid of me and marry that harlot, Urvi's friend. I don't even want to take her name."

"I'll talk to him and probably donate something for his election fund. What do you think about the idea?"

Chewing her lips, she shrugged.

"May I leave now? I have a meeting with our Japanese investors. Will you be okay? Rest today. I'll see you tomorrow at the office."

Vandana nodded, another tear escaping from her eye. Vikram wiped it from her cheek, kissed her temple, and left.

October 8th

"I can't believe this!" Vikram threw the reports and they landed at Esha's feet. "I can't even get a single error-free document between the three of you? Why do I pay you guys so much if I have to proofread everything?"

The three of them stood in front of him, in his office, getting grilled for something for which Esha was responsible. He had been blasting them for the past five minutes and she hadn't been able to get a word in between his tirades.

Esha had typed the report in which she had missed a couple of points and misspelled a few words. The word processor did not throw the error for obvious reasons. 'Manager' had become 'Manger', 'their' she had typed as 'there', and some more.

Twice she told him that the report was done by her, hoping he would take the hint and dismiss the other two. But no. Maria fidgeted, tired of standing, Esha guessed. And Koel shot daggers at her.

"Please don't justify." He yelled when she tried to apologize once again. He was past caring and paced the floor, the cigarette ash dotting the carpet.

Koel smirked. The smoke, as usual, tortured Esha. Then the door opened.

Vikram pivoted. "Can't you bloody knock?"

"I have to talk to Esha and you." Nikhil's tone, although quieter, matched the seriousness in his eyes.

Something in Nikhil's voice penetrated Vikram's haze of anger. He nodded and dismissed the other two.

"Where did you go today in the afternoon?" Nikhil's hands fisted at his sides as he turned to Esha. "And why were you not there with him?"

"I... afternoon. He had gone...?" Her eyes widened.

"Vikram, of all the irresponsible..."

"Cut it out, Nick. Jay was with me. It's over and done with." Vikram lit another cigarette and moved to the glass wall.

"You didn't even take the other vehicle with you. By the time they were informed, you were already at Vandana's place. How could you forget?"

Vikram whirled and spread his hand. "Nothing happened. I'm here, am I not? In one piece."

A pulse ticked on Nikhil's jaw as he glared at Vikram.

Vikram sighed. "Next time, I'll take care."

"Next time? Next time? Last week also you said the same thing. Have you no care? I'm leaving no stone unturned for this and you are behaving so recklessly. What if something happens to you? How will I show my face to the world, to your mother?"

"Fine, I will give you in writing that if anything happens to me, no one is to be held responsible."

"This is ridiculous." Nikhil banged his fist on the credenza beside him. The Buddha bust rattled precariously, then settled. He turned to Esha. "Did I not tell you to stick to him like glue?"

She wanted to say 'yes sir' but kept silent. Her hands went behind her back subconsciously and she stared at the painting on the front wall. He was right, she had been given her orders and had failed to follow them.

Nikhil sighed and raked his hair with his fingers. "Esha, you may leave."

"Fine, I made a mistake," Vikram began the moment Esha closed the door behind her. "It was just that I can't think straight when mom or *di* is in distress."

Nikhil sighed and nodded, knowing at best that this was the only apology he would get.

"Any update from Uday?" Vikram asked.

"Yeah, they are questioning anyone they can get their hands on. One of the parking guys is missing. Uday's team is trying to track him down. Meanwhile Jindal, Viraj, and their close confidantes are under surveillance. The illegal arms dealers in Delhi are being tracked. The bastard has sneaked off into his burrow like a coward rat he is."

"I can't think of a single incident or person whom I have offended to the extent that he could be after my life."

"We'll figure this out, don't worry," Nikhil said as he moved towards the door.

⊶⧫⊷

OUTHOUSE, SETHS' RESIDENCE, MUMBAI
8TH OCTOBER, 9:30 PM

The pressure cooker whistled again. Esha switched off the stove and attacked the onion she was slicing as if it were Vikram and Nikhil's egos. She simmered along with the rice and the vegetables she cooked. Was she supposed to learn shorthand in a day? It wasn't as if she had never been reprimanded. In the army, they were punished for anything and everything. What she didn't like was the way Vikram had done it in front of that smirking Koel.

And Nikhil! What did he think of himself? Was she supposed to be omniscient? Vikram had stormed out without his laptop and she had assumed he must have gone to a conference room or somewhere in the building. How was she supposed to know that he had left the office premises with only Jay to guard him? She could ask Jay to inform her if Vikram pulled this kind of a stunt again. But that would blow her cover. Goddamn!

Wiping the tears resulting from cutting the onion, she stood in front of the mini fridge contemplating the flavor of the yoghurt for dinner, when someone knocked at her door. She frowned. Was she getting the fabulous dinner again?

She opened the door and found the object of her fury standing outside, the dinner tray appearing so out of place in his hands. He hadn't change out of his formal suit, but there was no trace of anger as if the episode of the afternoon had been a dream. Her heart began its maddening beat and her nostrils twitched. But the amusement fled from his face when he laid eyes on her.

"Are you crying?" Vikram scowled.

"Of course not! I never cry." What a ludicrous thought!

"Never?" He smiled and glanced down at the tray.

"I've made my dinner," she said making no move to take the tray.

He took a deliberate in-your-face step forward with the tray against her stomach, forcing her to move back. Keeping the tray on the coffee table, he looked around leisurely. The room appeared smaller and somewhat cozy. The sliver of awareness ran through her again. She stopped fighting her body's reaction to him and sighed.

"Is the room to your liking?"

"Yes, thank you."

He picked up the novel she had been reading the night before, from the bed.

"Mr. Seth?" Esha didn't want him peeking into her personal life.

"I've come here to apologize."

Her eyes widened, for he didn't look the least bit contrite. In fact, after uttering those words, he kept the book down and moved towards the kitchenette.

"What's cooking?"

'*My peace of mind,*' she wanted to say but stayed silent.

He lifted the cooker lid and sniffed. "Smells okay, looks... um... unappetizing." And to her chagrin, he took a spoonful and ate her veg *khichdi*. "Not bad. But we are supposed to feed you. Have meals at home, it'll be easier for *dada*, he is getting old."

"Thank you. I can manage."

"I said I'm sorry." He moved towards the coffee table with lazy steps and picked up the transmitter-receiver set Nikhil had given her.

"Hey Major, have you eaten?" Nikhil spoke first and poked his head in later. "Oh... Vikram. You have already brought a tray... good, good." He glanced at Vikram then at her, a funny, almost indecipherable expression on his face.

"Yeah... and E... Major refuses my offer to eat at home."

"Why is it so, E-Major? I also eat there."

"That too, when I have apologized."

"You? Apologized?" Nikhil's eyebrows shot up, then recovered. "I too came to say sorry."

Esha glanced from one friend to the other, playing verbal hockey and—she was damn sure—they were amusing themselves at her expense. And what was the deal about 'E-Major'? Keeping her face blank, she went to the door and held it open. "Good night."

"Fine. See you tomorrow." Nikhil retreated as he had come.

She looked at Vikram who was still holding the transmitter, watching her with narrowed eyes.

"Is something going on between the two of you?" he said casually.

"Something going on?" She frowned.

"Yeah... I hope I'm not poaching on your time together." He jerked a thumb towards the door.

"I don't know about Nick, but you are definitely poaching on MY time, Mr. Seth." She clenched her teeth.

"Vikram."

"Huh?"

"Call me Vikram," he said, looking at her in his patented way, focusing on each feature, lingering on her lips a moment too long.

Her already pounding heart jumped to her throat.

"Good night, Major. See you at breakfast." He kept the transmitter down and moved towards the door, then turned. "Oh yes... you can use the gym at home. It's in the basement. The entrance is from the back and it'll open with your card and thumb imprint." He saluted and left, leaving her all the more perplexed with his changing moods.

⸻◦✦◦⸻

SUBURBS, MUMBAI
8TH OCTOBER, 9:30 PM

She sat looking outside the window, thinking about him. Surely he was supposed to come today. She hoped she hadn't mixed up the dates again. But he'll remember, she was sure. He never forgot anything. He was a king—so smart, so handsome.

Look at the palace he had provided for her... all virginal white.

She had been a virgin that first night and had stained his pristine white sheets. He had been so patient with her, soothing her, telling her not to worry about the sheets. He had changed them and helped her get clean again. Then they had made love again and Anna came into existence. Their child... Born out of their love in—

Where was Anna born? She didn't remember. When did he see her and their child for the first time? Was he there in the hospital? The memory refused to surface. Where was her baby? Panic numbed her.

Confused, she looked around and saw their daughter sleeping in the pink crib. The fear receded. Oh God! Why was she so dull-headed all the time? She peeked inside the crib.

Anna was so much like him—beautiful, pretty, and always cheerful. Their little girl was so well-behaved, she never threw tantrums. She was sure her baby doll would follow her father's footsteps and graduate from Harvard.

Why wasn't he coming? The sun was going down. Wasn't it time for him to come? She was beginning to get the jitters again.

What had he promised her? Was he supposed to come today or tomorrow? She had forgotten again.

Anna began crying, probably sensing her distress. Poor baby. She picked her up from the crib and crooned a lullaby. Her voice soothed the baby as well as her own soul. Her voice was divine, he had said once.

"He should have come by now! Why the delay?" She wondered, but the next moment she admonished herself. He was a busy man, a king. She should be the one supporting him rather than expecting him to come running to her. But she wasn't a stupid woman. She understood him and his obligations. Yes, she did.

The baby was asleep.

She lay her down in the crib, failing to acknowledge the open blue plastic eyes.

⸻◈⸻

PART TWO: SYMPHONY

October 11th

Esha finished sweeping the outer room and took the scanner into Vikram's office. It had been three days and she had fallen into the planned routine. Nikhil had arranged for sophisticated scanners for bugs and bombs, which were handy, concealed in a TV remote, but she had to be discreet. She had another half an hour before anyone arrived.

The scent of Vikram's unmistakable brand of tobacco lingered in the room, not acute enough to bother her allergies but sufficient to remind her that this was his space, every article unmistakably masculine and expensive. Touching the objects and things that he had used and would be using brought an unexpected intimacy to the whole exercise every day.

She caressed the bright onyx paperweight. He had been holding it the day he had told her not to stand in the military stance, suggesting she should fiddle with something to keep her hands occupied, worried that she might blow her cover. She smiled at her own stupidity and scanned the credenza.

On her second night on the job, he had broken the formal distance between them for the first time, bringing her the dinner. Was he attracted to her too? Or was she reading too much into it? No. She hadn't imagined his lingering gaze on her lips. Or maybe, he was making up for his outburst earlier in the office that afternoon.

After that night, they hadn't had an opportunity for a personal conversation. Partly because of his busy schedule and partly because she made sure that they were never alone.

Using the legitimate excuse of leaving early for the office, she had avoided any direct conversation. She completed her gym session by five in the morning. Striking a deal with Kishore *dada*, she ate breakfast at the kitchen counter. And Vikram would always be busy on his phone during their commute back home, so much so that he often had his dinner while working in his den at home. Even Nikhil had been out of station for the past two days. So effectively, she had lived in peace for the past three days.

A muted click of someone entering the outer room brought her back from her reflections. Keeping the paperweight back, she resumed scanning, not bothered with the intrusion since she had locked the door so that no one could come inside when she checked and sanitized the office rooms.

The person crossed the outer room and tried to unlock the office. The door handle twisted many a time. Esha smiled when she heard Koel's muffled curse. She was one nosy busybody.

"Why do you always come so early in the morning?" Koel blasted the question the moment Esha stepped out of his room. "And why did you lock the room?"

"You are early."

"Why do YOU come early? To sweep and mop the office?" Koel smirked.

Esha chuckled. "Yeah... in fact you are right."

"So where is your broom?"

"I don't need a broom, I have... what do you call it... a wand."

"Bitch..." Koel muttered, pivoting towards her desk.

"More like a witch." Vikram's deep baritone cut into their conversation.

Koel whirled around and began blabbering. "Oh my God, I'm so sorry sir, we were just fooling around, weren't we, Esha?" All flustered, Koel stood there wringing her hands with her gaze bouncing from Vikram to Esha, but neither of them paid any attention to her predicament.

"Good morning," Esha said, unable to break the eye contact, "Board meeting today," she finally blurted.

He blinked and stepped forward. "Yeah, the board meeting. So, have you waved your wand for it or not?" he asked crossing the room to enter his office.

"Maria will be waving hers," she said causing him to chuckle.

Leaning on his door, he looked back and threw a devastating smile at her before barricading himself in the room for the day.

⸺⸺◆⸺⸺

Esha thanked her lucky charms that Maria's maternity leave would start after the board meeting. She didn't have a clue about logistics and Koel had refused to help her in anything. Apparently, the seating in the board room was fixed and the stationery and refreshments were to be arranged according to each individual's preferences. Quirks of rich people.

Esha had sanitized the room in the morning and had done another check after Maria left to bring her laptop. On a spur of the moment, she crouched under the table for a last-minute check as Vikram entered with his mother, Maria close behind them.

"Ms. Sinha, are you waving your magic wand under the table?" Vikram said as he entered the plush room.

Scoundrel. He knew what she was doing and yet he had to bring everyone's attention to her. "I'm sorry, I dropped my pen." Esha stood up twirling the pen in her left hand, keeping the right behind her back. He grinned at her, throwing a fleeting glance at her right hand.

"Mom, meet Ms. Esha Sinha, she will be working with me temporarily, in place of Maria."

Thankfully, his mother didn't expect a handshake. Mrs. Seth tilted her head, smiled perfunctorily, and took her seat adjacent to Vikram, who sat at the head of the table.

For Esha, it was a tableau unfolding as the chairs of the conference room were taken one by one. She had read about the people in attendance, but in reality, they brought their personality along, filling the gaps in their respective dossiers.

"Good morning, everyone." His sister, Vandana, addressed everyone in the room. She was a beautiful lady, though she wasn't as tall as her mom or Vikram. She had an aura of vulnerability around her that inspired one to protect her. Her husband and aspiring MP, Gautam

Jindal, was tall and charismatic, complementing his wife. But it seemed there was trouble brewing in their marriage, for sitting opposite each other, neither of them acknowledged the other.

"Where's Viraj?" Mrs. Seth asked.

"Must be lying in some hell hole... the good for nothing..." Vandana muttered.

"It's okay, Vandana." Mrs. Seth cut her short.

"Yes, I know ma, we have to maintain the decorum. I'm sorry. But why always us? Shouldn't he show some sense of responsibility?"

"Anyway, let's begin. I have a busy day today," Mrs. Seth said.

There were a couple of directors from outside the family present as advisors without any voting rights. Esha braced herself for two hours of utter boredom, where everything discussed would be beyond her understanding. Numbers and math had never been her favorite subjects. Thankfully, Maria's and her own seats were in one corner, behind the head of the table.

The door of the room slammed open after they had discussed the first item on the agenda.

"Hi guys, did you miss me?" A man stood at the threshold, smiling insolently as he scanned the room. His gaze settled on Vikram, who sat watching him passively. "Aah, everyone is angry except my little, intelligent brother, Vikramaditya Seth. It seems I'm not sufficiently late." He was a tall and lanky man, stylishly dressed in the height of fashion. His daring stance and veiled insults had no effect on Vikram. Rotating the laser pointer in his hand, Vikram studied the man in silence.

"Sit down, Viraj. I have another meeting after this," Mrs. Seth said.

"Oh... my dear respected *chachiji*!" He rushed towards her and made a play at touching her feet, but he didn't even bend down. "What would we have been but for you?"

"Cut the crap, Viraj," Jindal said, grinning at him.

"Did you like it?" Viraj grinned, displaying a perfect set of white teeth as he sat beside Jindal. Viraj was Vikram's cousin on his father's side. Viraj's father had been a drug addict and had died of drug overdose ten years back. Viraj worked under Vikram, as per the will of their grandfather, and handled Seth's chain of hotels.

"Shall we begin, ladies and gentlemen?" Vikram nodded at the people at the table.

Everyone gave their status and agreed on the next quarter's targets. Watching Vikram tackle each person was a revelation. He would see the loopholes in the business strategy and discussion that no one otherwise could point out.

The meeting went smoothly till the time it was Viraj's turn. He was managing their chain of five-star hotels spread all over the country. Vikram vetoed investing another hundred crores in the hotels that Viraj had suggested. Esha had glazed over a major part of the discussion, so she peeped at Maria's screen for the missing notes.

"Why?" Viraj stood up to bang the table.

Startled, Esha looked up from her screen. Viraj's pale complexion had gone red, his hands fisted by his sides.

She scanned the other faces around the table. Jindal looked positively delighted as if he was waiting for an interesting drama to unfold. Everybody else looked bored, already fed up of the theatrics maybe, with the exception of Vandana. She was eyeing Viraj with a loathing that bordered on murderous rage. The pen in her hand was drilling a hole in the white notepad that was embossed with her name.

"The investment will bring down the share prices. Any improvement done for the hotels has to be earned from the business, not taken from the shareholders," Vikram said.

Although Esha heard Vikram's cold and correct response, she was totally besotted with Vandana's reaction. Vandana's face went soft, filled with pride as she transferred her glance to Vikram. It was apparent that she adored her younger brother.

"But you know that tourism has been bad this year."

"A risk that looms every year, and something that you have to manage, Viraj." Vikram switched off the wall projection screen. "Since everything has been covered for the next quarter, I think we can adjourn the meeting. Viraj, you and I will continue this discussion in private." Vikram stood up, signaling the end of the meeting.

"Whatever you want to say, say it in front of everyone. I don't give a damn!" Viraj clenched his jaw, clearly upset at the authoritative tone Vikram had used with him.

"I don't think I can spare any more time," Mrs. Seth cut in with her crisp response even as she and her secretary shuffled and collected their files and belongings.

"No one goes till the time I say so!" Viraj yelled.

"Viraj, don't create a scene." Jindal held Viraj's arm.

"Thank you, everyone." Mrs. Seth left the room with her assistant.

The other members too followed her out except for Jindal and Vandana, who sat watching the drama unfold—Jindal, with a faint smile, and Vandana, with wary contempt.

"You can't control us like this, as if we don't have any brains. Every time..." Viraj's hands fisted.

"Maria, please go home, you look tired. Esha and I'll manage." Vikram closed his notebook. Maria nodded and left the room with her files.

"I'll—"

"Viraj, I said we'll discuss this in private." Vikram picked up his notebook.

Esha noticed Nikhil entering the room and taking a position with his back to the closed door. No one paid any attention to him.

All of a sudden, Viraj stepped forward and rammed a fist into Vikram's jaw. Startled, Esha stood up, and the notebook on her lap smashed to the floor. Vandana gasped. Nikhil rushed forward and grabbed Viraj's arms from behind. Viraj struggled, unsuccessfully, against Nikhil's vice-like grip. Vikram took out a handkerchief and wiped the blood off his lips.

Jindal stood up, shaking his head. "Come on Viraj, boy. Don't get all heated up. Nothing comes out of anger. Nick, leave him."

Nikhil left him but planted himself between Vikram and Viraj.

"I'll not forget this." Viraj spat on the floor and glared at Vikram and Nikhil.

"Nothing new. We'll discuss your plan after you have cooled down. Ask for an appointment."

Esha couldn't understand why Vikram was hell-bent on goading him. Though nothing showed on his face, she gathered that he was livid with Viraj. She picked up her notebook. It had switched off and the screen was cracked.

"You know Vikram, you shouldn't pick a fight with any and everyone," Jindal drawled, dragging Viraj out of the room. "Someday you may cross the line."

Vandana scowled and snorted, glancing at her husband.

"He is bad news." Vandana took a step closer to Vikram and peered at his face.

"Don't worry. I'm fine." Vikram smiled and she beamed at him. Cautioning him to take care once again, she left the room.

"I have to go to Delhi. They have a lead." Nikhil said as the door swung close and the three of them were alone in the room.

Vikram, who was nodding absentmindedly as he scanned the project reports they had discussed last, stopped to stare at Nikhil. "What?"

"They have a lead. Uday has tracked down someone who had let the vehicle out of the parking,"

"Be careful, Nick. Don't go overboard," Vikram said.

Esha frowned at his words but masked her expression as Nikhil turned to look at her.

"Xena, you'll have to manage with Jay. He knows the operations in the office and the general protocol."

"Don't worry, I've read them too. We'll manage."

JINDAL'S ELECTION OFFICE, MUMBAI
11TH OCTOBER, 9:00 PM

While going back home, Vikram instructed Jay to take them to Jindal's office. "You stay here," Vikram told Esha when she made a move to follow him. "This is private," he muttered.

But Esha had no intention of listening to him and followed him inside. Vikram sensed her presence when they were halfway through the office, turned and glared at her. She straightened to her full height and met his glance squarely. He pursed his lips then regarded the couple sitting at the corner desk, reading and cutting news items from the various newspapers and magazines scattered around, least bothered about the visitors.

Unwilling to make a scene, Vikram sighed and moved towards the inner office. The couple in the room, sitting on the wide office chair, broke apart hastily, as Vikram opened the door. The woman squealed and turned her back to them. They couldn't help but watch her button her blouse and re-wrap the sari around her. Without meeting their eyes, she left the room muttering something inaudibly to Jindal who, after the first stunned moment, sat smiling on the chair.

"Vikram, what an untimely entry! I expected you to follow the basic etiquettes of calling or knocking." He threw a cursory glance at Esha. "And what is your PA doing here? Are we going to have the minutes of our meeting recorded?"

He turned towards her. "Esha, wait outside," he instructed, then added, "Please."

Nodding, Esha scanned the room discretely and moved out closing the door behind her. The voices from the room could be heard, but she couldn't make out the conversation, which should be acceptable, she thought. She planted herself on a chair outside the door pretending to read the messages on her phone, alert in case of any unnatural sound or movement.

A few minutes later, a cold, unnatural wave of air caressed her nape, making her shiver. The couple at the desk had left, but Esha sensed she wasn't alone in the room. She looked around casually, but she could see no one. The feeling of being watched, however, intensified. She discreetly scanned the room for any hidden cameras but couldn't find any of those either. It wasn't surprising since there were too many objects in there that could be used to hide a small camera.

Someone was watching her, Esha was certain, maybe through a camera. She relaxed her demeanor without lowering her guard, even as she slipped her hand in the pocket and unclipped the safety latch on the gun.

⬥

JINDAL'S OFFICE, MUMBAI
11TH OCTOBER, 9:05 PM

Vikram relaxed in his chair and calmly looked at Jindal swiveling his chair, left to right. He was adept at waiting people out and Jindal was not a patient man.

"Okay, truce." Jindal stamped the table after a few minutes and went towards the bar. "What will you like to have?" He continued when Vikram didn't reply. "I'm not having an affair. You know an affair would be an unnecessary encumbrance for me at this time. These are just a few transitory people who need something from me, a little favor here and a little there. You know..."

"Don't you think it is an insult to my sister?"

"Aah... your sister... beautiful, elusive... your holier than thou sister." Jindal raised his glass in a silent toast. "Vikram since you have seen what you have seen, and since your sister has complained to you about my indiscretion, I think it's better if you know the complete story." He waved his hand around. "And I'm not justifying or giving excuses. I'm telling you the facts of our lives, your darling sister's life." He paused to take a sip of the drink he had prepared. "She doesn't allow me, her husband, in her bed. In fact, I'm not allowed to enter her room without her permission, for the last... the last nine-ten months or so..."

"You are lying."

"Oh please, Vikram! We have been married for twelve long years, and you know I have worshipped the grounds she has walked on. But I guess feelings change. She has taken an averse dislike to me, and I don't know the reason. I tried to sort out the problem, I did try, but I couldn't solve. And a man... a man has his needs. I don't need to explain that to you, m'dear."

"Why didn't you talk to my mother or me, then? Right at the beginning?"

"Pride. That is also an emotion to which you will relate well."

"I can't. Not in this case."

"Then you better get the hell out of here before I lose my cool. I don't have the time for you or your sister and her theatrics."

"You are forgetting that I can lose my cool too. The only thing that stops me is the values of my family."

"Oh yes! Your family and their lofty standards. No one can do... no let me state this correctly... no one should do anything wrong that will adversely affect the honor of Vikramaditya Seth Sr's family!"

Jindal was now talking about Vikram's father's principles in life, but Vikram didn't feel the need to defend his father. His father had always done right by everyone.

"And if anything goes wrong, brush it under the carpet. For, God forbid, if the world sees it, any of the ugly truths of Seth's family, lightning will strike." Jindal waved his hands in the air and cackled with senseless mirth.

Vikram watched him with uncharacteristic detachment—somehow, he had never warmed up to the man. The tension of the impending elections was making its presence felt. Tiredness and age showed clearly on the wrinkles around his eyes and mouth.

Jindal now struggled to control his laughter, even as tears streamed down his face making him look like a shadow of his elegant self, the image he portrayed in front of the media. Vikram gritted his jaw, tired of the whole mess.

"My father had a code of honor and lived by it all his life. But he never said that you should stay in a relationship that is not working after you have done everything in your power to mend it. He never opposed my divorce.

Not that I'm hinting at yours. You have chosen to stay married because you want to portray a false image of an upright family man for your ambitions of becoming the Chief Minister of the state now, and maybe the Prime Minister later."

Jindal smirked and took another swig from his glass.

Vikram was well aware of Jindal's campaign not going in the direction he wished and of his frustration thereby. The people Vikram had employed to track the election campaign and the preliminary results had briefed him about Jindal's not-so-bright prospects.

"Do you need more money?" Vikram asked him pointedly.

"Oh come on, Vikram, don't behave like your father, always trying to buy my affection for your sister." Jindal gulped his drink in one go and smashed the glass on the fake electrical chimney. "I have enough money of my own."

"Just to let you know that you have my blessings for whatever decision you both take about your relationship. Please sort this out with her." Vikram didn't want to interfere in their personal matters. "But I won't tolerate the hitting again." His tone had taken a hard glint. It might be their personal matter, their relationship, but there was no way he'd tolerate Jindal abusing his sister— physically or mentally.

"What do you mean? I have never hit a woman in my life." Jindal spread his hands.

Vikram had come to the end of his patience as Jindal delivered the lie with a high dosage of drama. He didn't have the patience for this anymore. "Just remember this my dear *jijaji*, zero tolerance if you touch my sister again," he spat and left, leaving the man sweating.

Esha stood up as she heard the door to Jindal's office open. Vikram came out with his eyebrows furrowed and hands fisted. She followed him out and the hair at her nape prickled again as the car passed a uniformed man at the gate. She couldn't see his face clearly under the dim lamp post with the cap pulled low over his forehead but filed his partial visual statistics in her brain. Just in case.

The moment the car exited the gate, Vikram flicked a switch and a glass screen came up cutting Jay from them at the back seat. "I told you to stay in the car." He sounded a bit like an old military general but didn't care. As it is, it was embarrassing that she had witnessed his family's mess.

"I have been told to apply my own discretion in this job."

"He is my brother-in-law."

"In my eyes, everyone's a suspect. I'm not buying the terrorist story."

Vikram glared at her but she met his anger with an unflinching gaze, her chin raised. She was challenging his take on the matter but not overtly. His anger dissipated rapidly looking at her calm and serene face. What did it take to rile her? Expelling a long breath, he raked his hair with his fingers.

"Defiance suits you." He smiled. Somehow, it didn't matter that she had seen one of his family members in a shameful act. She was not the one to judge anyone, ever. He was damn sure her mind never ran on those lines.

"Were you always this indomitable and insolent or is it just me who brings out these qualities in you?"

"We all have to do what we have to do."

"I have been to Jindal's office countless times in the past twenty odd years and have never been threatened."

"Feelings change. Motives change. You have been shot at also for the first time."

"No, not the first time."

She stared at him, genuinely shocked that she didn't know this detail of his life.

"What? You don't know that I had been kidnapped and shot at when I was small?"

That elicited a reaction. Her lips parted a bit.

Vikram grinned, curbing the sudden urge to kiss her mouth close. "Great, at least the media gag worked on that episode of my life."

Frowning, she turned to gaze out of the car.

He waited for her to get over the shock and ask him the details on the kidnapping, but she kept looking out. Though it was one of the episodes he was not keen to relive, he had thought he would tell her if she asked nicely.

She turned towards him.

He waited expectantly for the questions.

"Nick should look into the staff on Jindal's payroll too," she said instead.

She was one stubborn woman with a one-track mind. He had got under her skin today, and he was sure he would figure her out by the time this bodyguard business was over and she stopped looking at him as an assignment.

He sighed and flicked the button that brought the privacy screen down. They were about to reach home.

SETHS' RESIDENCE, MUMBAI
11TH OCTOBER, 10:30 PM

Esha entered the kitchen by-passing the dining room as she had been doing for most of the days and spotted Kishore *dada* sprinkling salt on the salad.

"Need any help?" she asked.

He smiled, shaking his head. It had become their ritual. He was a man of few words, but he surprised her by adding, "*Baba* has asked you to join him in the dining room."

She sighed, as her mind raced helter-skelter to come up with a valid excuse without any success. "I don't feel like having dinner." She threw the words, picked up a banana from the fruit basket, and hurried out the back door before he could respond.

Putting on some light music on her phone, Esha took out the flavored yoghurt from the mini-fridge of the apartment and settled on the bed with her unfinished novel.

Someone knocked. Her heart froze. Why couldn't he leave her alone? She turned the phone down and switched off the lights. He would think she was asleep. It was a sheer juvenile reaction, but she didn't want to face him. It had been a long day.

To her surprise, the door clicked open.

"Hi, I've brought you some aspirins," he continued as she lay face-down on the bed. "Esha, come on... I know you aren't asleep, I heard the music."

That did it. She switched on the bedside lamp and sat on the bed with her legs crossed. "Why can't you take no for an answer?"

"I want to talk to you. As it is I don't get time." Vikram placed the tray laden with dishes and plates on the bed.

"Can't you take a hint?"

"No." He picked up a plate and served. "I have to go to mother's tomorrow and to the CNBC event one of the days next week. And I don't like eating alone. No, that's a lie. I want to eat with you today."

"How did you enter my room?"

"Magic." Grinning, he waved the magnetic card in front of her face before slipping it in the back pocket of his jeans.

He would have the master key, of course, Esha thought mentally chiding herself. Why didn't she think about that? She should have bolted the door, she realized as she glanced at him. He had taken a shower and changed into casual clothes. Damp hair curled under the collar of his black t-shirt. The pulsating tingle she had been experiencing since the time he had entered the room, changed into sizzling alternating-currents. She dropped her gaze to the phone in her hand.

"Major?"

She looked up from the phone to find him holding the dinner plate for her.

"I'm not hungry."

"Don't be silly, you need sustenance. I know how hard you workout each day, and I also know you skip lunch because you can't leave your vigil outside my office. Don't remain hungry on my account, it makes me feel guilty. I'll go once we have eaten. And I promise to leave you alone if you give me an honest answer to a question."

That intrigued her enough to take the plate. "What's the question?"

"Why are you avoiding me?" Loading his own plate, Vikram sat on one of the easy chairs near the bed and began eating. He watched her as she ate. He did right to bring the dinner to her. She was ravenous.

"So, why are you avoiding me?" He repeated the question.

She glanced at him from the plate, again with that bland school-teacher look.

"I never thought you'd be a coward," he said.

«I'm not.»

"Not what? A coward?"

"Not avoiding. I have to start my day early."

"Come on, you have to start only fifteen minutes ahead of me. But you are going to the gym at five and having your breakfast at six. What should I construe from all this?"

"You are not supposed to interpret anything from my routine. It's my time and I have full right to do as I please when I'm not on duty."

He couldn't understand his own growing schoolboy fascination with her. The barrage of words and pronounced lisp indicated she was irked, but her eyes still remained placid. He wanted to ignite some emotion within her, even if it was a negative one. It was probably because he had been without a woman for a long time, he took a lame guess. "Whoa... slow down. I meant it in a friendly way. I'm not complaining about your work."

"I'm not a friendly person."

This was new! He detected a kind of forlorn edge to her tone. It was uttered in a low, resigned manner as if it was her fate more than her nature.

"I don't believe it. Everyone's friendly, given the right group, atmosphere, and circumstances."

Esha kept quiet and continued to eat, wondering how to answer him without prolonging the discussion.

"Esha?"

"I have no intention of starting a WhatsApp group with you."

"Though I have never used WhatsApp, I think it'll be hilarious to have a group of two people. Can't we just talk? Face-to-face, without the interference of technology."

She glanced at him. He sounded amused as well as earnest. For a moment, she was tempted to be honest as he had suggested, but that would complicate things.

Maybe he would laugh her views off, or maybe he would think she was ready for a fling as the other women around him. Wouldn't that take her into the category of the Koels and Karismas of the world? She knew there was something wrong between Karisma and him. One showdown, though behind the closed doors of his office, had happened on Tuesday.

Was he looking for a short-term fling with her? She was a safe bet, wasn't she? After the assignment, she would go her way. She was his safest bet since she wouldn't even stay back in the same city.

"I don't find it easy to mingle with strangers."

He smiled and took a bite from his plate without taking his eyes off her. "You are such a big liar, Major. Do you have a photograph of you in the uniform?"

"No." She scowled. "Why?"

"I'm curious to know if you look sexier in a uniform. You don't have it with you?" Taking a bite, he grinned then added. "Not even on WhatsApp?"

"I have answered your question. Now please leave."

"That wasn't an honest answ—" His phone rang, interrupting their conversation. He sighed looking at the caller ID, but let the mobile ring. "I need to take this call. Thanks for the company. We'll continue this discussion some other time. See you at breakfast tomorrow."

He simply gathered their plates and took them out with him. She hadn't ever expected him to clear the plates. Esha stared at the door he had closed behind him, marveling at the multi-millionaire who didn't hesitate to do simple chores so that he could help his fifty-odd-years old servant who had gout. He could have left it for her to clean, after all, he had brought the dinner and she worked for him.

No doubt he was a charismatic man. And she had come across many such appealing men in the army. In fact, she had been involved with one. All the girls envied the attention Samar lavished on her.

During the NSG training too, she was the only woman in their group, not that it ever got her an advantage from the officers or the fellow cadets. Esha didn't expect anything else either. She shared the same bunkers and used the common bathroom. She had seen well-built, magnificent male anatomy and was no prissy female. At her age and in her line of work, she was expected to keep her emotions tightly leashed.

But then, what was it about Vikram Seth that pulled her like a nail to a magnet? She slammed the book down. Goddamn!

A DESERTED WAREHOUSE, PATPARGANJ, NEW DELHI
11TH OCTOBER, 11:30 PM

"Aaahh... hhh." Sitting on the chair, the thin man doubled up in pain. "Fuck... fuck," he hissed and struggled against the grip.

The masked man standing behind him gave another twist to his arm and the man on the chair whimpered, tears now flowing freely from one of his swollen eyes. Standing in front of him, Nikhil stared at him blankly from behind his mask.

"Please... Please... I don't know anything. I swear on my dead mother." He pulled in a deep breath and yanked at his captor again.

The dim light from the low wattage bulb hanging from the ceiling threw sinister shadows in the room.

"One word... One name Munna... and you know this pain will end," Nikhil drawled in a low menacing tone pulling on the latex gloves. Munna started to shiver now. "Else you will come to know I am capable of pulling out each of your nails... slowly... till you sing." He brought out a plier from the tool bag on the floor. "And, let me also tell you that this place is soundproof."

"Who are you guys? What have I done?" Munna whispered.

"The good thing is that you haven't done anything so far, so I'm going to let you live, but the bad thing is that if you don't open your gab soon, I'm going to make sure that you beg for death," Nikhil hissed and punched him again.

"Ah... I don't know... aahhh." The aluminum chair clattered against the front wall and Munna landed on his face as Nikhil kicked the chair, blood spurting from Munna's nose. It looked like he had broken a tooth. Munna turned around, his single eye widened in fear, and slowly shifted back to the wall. Nikhil stood ten paces away from him, opening and closing the pliers.

"Listen, we are not the police. No law binds us. We are beyond anyone." The other masked man positioned himself beside Munna and pulled him up.

"A woman... It was a woman's voice over the phone, she called... and she told me to leave the car in the parking!" he wailed, when Nikhil took a step towards him.

"Now you are acting intelligent Munna. Her name?" Nikhil clicked his fingers and Munna jerked in attention. "Quick... good... her name?"

"I don't knoooow!" Munna cried. "I swear I don't know."

"I'm not going to ask again." Nikhil took Munna's hand in his, pried open his fist, and held a nail with the plier.

"Debbie... Debbie... She dances in the dance bar in Mumbai," Munna moaned, "But, don't hurt her... Please don't hurt her! She is just a pawn..."

"How was the payment done?"

"All cash... Delivered at my doorstep in a can of milk. I don't know anything more... Please... Aah... Please, I'm telling you the truth."

"Of course you are..." Releasing his finger from the plier, Nikhil put his mouth near Munna's ear and whispered. "Remember, if you have lied I'll catch you again. You might fool the police but you can't hide from me."

Assured that he had put the fear of the unknown in Munna's mind, Nikhil nodded at his companion. The other man held a wad of chloroform on Munna's face and Munna went limp.

⸻⟡⸻

October 12th

'Waiting.' Esha's stomach went topsy turvy as she read the single word text from Vikram at seven thirty the next morning. It was a Saturday and Esha knew that excusing herself on account of work couldn't save her this time.

Still, she didn't want to be a part of moments that included his private life. But this was one job where there was no space for privacy or the luxury of me-time, and she couldn't hide forever.

She would have to go or Vikram would taunt her again. Well, she had some ideas to make sure that the conversation remained on professional grounds. Unplugging the Bluetooth from the charger, she pushed it in the jacket pocket. The jacket had become a necessity—she felt more confident with the gun close at hand after the evening at Jindal's office.

In the dark of the night, the enclosed premises looked regal. But during the day, the light added to the persona of the old bungalows in Mumbai. With creepers winding over the new age white metal windows, the three-story building was like a bridge between the old and the new generation.

The massive main door was slightly ajar. Esha took the five steps up the patio leisurely and entered. Nikhil had given her the basic layout of the three floors of the house so she knew her way around but was not prepared for the stark, contemporary décor that looked straight out of a magazine. With three generations living in the house, she had expected ornate glass windows and heavy teak furniture. On the contrary, she found nothing but chrome, steel, and ivory upholstery. It looked elegant yet lifeless as if no one lived there—a house without a soul.

The muted tinkle of cutlery coming from the left of the living room disabused her of the hope that they would have finished and she would have the dining room to herself.

"Hi! Good morning, Xena." Nikhil spotted her first.

"Good morning. That was quick, Nick. When did you come back?" she asked. Without even scanning the room, she sensed Vikram standing by the window.

"Took the late night flight. Come sit, I've just started. Couldn't resist the *methi parathas,*" Nikhil said, digging into his plate.

Esha nodded and glanced at Vikram. He was wearing a designer Chinese-collar linen shirt over jeans, fit on his lean length and suiting him perfectly. His hair, still wet from the shower, clung to his skull. She knew it would soon fall over his brow by the time breakfast was over. Thankfully, he wasn't smoking.

As she reluctantly brought her gaze to meet his eyes, he smiled and gestured towards the buffet spread on the table parallel to the dining table. With a slight nod, she took a plate from him. He served himself after dutifully waiting for her to fill her plate—like a host would for a guest.

They sat at one end of the dining table that could seat twelve people, with him sitting at the head of the table and Nikhil to his right. After a slight hesitation, she chose the seat on his left keeping her eyes on the plate. Nikhil was busy reading the newspaper, so the responsibility of starting a conversation was left on either Vikram or her.

Esha sighed and started with the topic she had planned to discuss. "I read the Delhi police's investigation reports you had given me, Nick. The sniper left at the Golf Club was customized. The man, it seems, is a leftie."

"Yeah..."

"Or maybe he had two rifles and was trying to mislead," Esha said.

Both of them stopped eating and glanced at her.

"What about—"

The house bell rang interrupting her chain of thoughts. After a few seconds, the double-door opened and everyone turned towards the intrusion.

"Hey, everyone!" Karisma stood at the entrance in her body-hugging lounge suit, looking like a model out of a magazine. She raised her fine eyebrows as she spotted Esha.

"Hi Karisma, come and have some *parathas*." Nikhil invited her when Vikram didn't.

"Thanks but no, I don't endorse such heavy stuff early in the morning. I have specifically come to meet you, Nick."

"Aha! A woman with a purpose. Bring it on!"

"I need your permission to go out for an evening with Vikram." Though she spoke to Nikhil, her eyes were on Vikram, who continued eating but observed the proceeding as if he was invisible.

It was hilarious to see Nikhil's expression—for once, words had failed him. He sat there with his mouth open and spoon held mid-air. Esha bit her cheek and glanced at Vikram who, to her mortification, was looking at her with an intent considering look. Her throat suddenly went dry and the room became silent, as she sensed the two pair of eyes at both of them. She picked up another spoonful of the scrambled eggs from her plate.

Nikhil coughed. "He is a free man, Karisma. You have my blessings."

"I have been given some other signal." Karisma now studied Esha with a penetrating look, thanks to the trouble-brewer sitting beside her. "We haven't met. Hi, I'm Karisma."

"Esha Sinha."

"Nick, please don't mind, your girlfriend?"

"Alas no! I have been asking her out since we have met. But no. No such luck."

Bemused, Esha couldn't help but look at him. She then sneaked a look at Vikram, who was now scowling at Nikhil and Karisma.

"I think I should be going." Esha stood up trying to end the awkward morning.

"No, no. Please sit, don't get up on my account, and finish your breakfast. Please." Karisma placed one hand on her shoulder and gently pushed her down. "Probably we should make this a double date, maybe then Vikram will find the courage to step out of the house."

"Karisma, don't you think you are being overly dramatic." The hand on the table fisted and the puckered skin of the scar became pink.

"Ah, finally! Finally, I get a reaction from you."

Esha couldn't fathom who was angrier, Vikram or Karisma. They glared at each other. Suddenly, he loosened his fist, smiled and said, "I think double date is a great idea."

Karisma inhaled.

"What do you think, Esha?" He touched Esha's hand on the table, which she withdrew on a split-second reflex. But the damage to her pulse had been done—it took off like a bullet, cutting off the oxygen to her lungs.

"Nick?" Vikram turned to Nikhil as if the idea had come from him.

Nikhil regarded him for a few pregnant seconds, then smiled. "As you wish my friend."

"I'm sorry, I don't want to go," Esha blurted.

"Coward," Vikram whispered, only for her ears.

Esha couldn't understand what he was playing at? He had had a falling out with his girlfriend, okay. But why was he dragging both of them into the mess? Scowling, she glared at Nikhil, who sat smiling, his eyes fixed on his plate.

"But you must. Don't be afraid, I'm with you."

Both men smiled as Karisma uttered the sentence. Oblivious to the undercurrents floating in the room, Karisma continued, "That's settled then. This evening we dine at the restaurant that I choose. I'll convey the venue in an hour. I'm counting on you, Nick." She gave a light hug to Vikram and, after placing an airy kiss on his cheek, she left.

"Well, if it's a free evening, I'd like to make my own plans," Esha announced.

"It's not a free evening. We'll be on duty, Xena," Nikhil corrected.

"No, you will not. You are going to enjoy the evening as my guests," Vikram said.

"Vikram…"

"For god's sake! Call the extra guards, do the sanitization, and then enjoy. Does that meet your approval?"

"If you are so bothered about my work-life balance, why don't you call her here?" Nikhil snapped.

"I don't want to. Come on, it's just one evening, *yaar*. When was the last time we shared a beer without any reason?"

Nikhil eventually gave in and nodded.

Esha again felt like an outsider, watching the play-off of genuine concern and affection they had for each other.

"Do you have something suitable to wear for the evening?" Nikhil asked her, as she stood up to go to her room.

"Is there a dress code?"

"Yeah… I mean, you never know. Depends on the restaurant she chooses. I'll let you know once she has decided."

"Thanks for tipping me off," Esha said but groaned silently at the thought of shopping for new clothes.

Esha needed a dress.

Nikhil had texted her the name of the restaurant. She used her afternoon off to buy something suitable for the evening, but there was nothing that could be called a dress and could also hide the gun on her person. Everything was either figure-hugging, short, or both. A gown was out of the question—she found them too constricting and was not confident that she would be able to do justice to the outfit.

In the end, she settled on a silver-sequined A-line mid-thigh skirt and a plain orange, layered georgette top. The under slip that came with the top had a pocket for holding a phone and some small accessories. Esha figured it was perfect enough for her to slip the gun into. The asymmetrical layers of the top would conceal the bulge and it would make for easier access as well.

The next step was to get the works done in the salon. She endured the two hours of torture, all the while praying to God to let her be born as a man in the next incarnation, in case she had to be born again.

She came back to her apartment and found two boxes kept on the table. Her first thought was to run and ask Nikhil for a bomb scanner, then remembered it wasn't possible for anyone to sneak in a virgin packet inside. She let out a breath of relief and picked up the card attached to one of the boxes.

'For today evening. Hope it meets your specifications.'
- VAS

The card fell from her hand. The note sounded literally impersonal, but for her it was as personal and intimate as one could get. No one had gifted her anything in her thirty-odd years on Earth. Samar had mentioned buying something for her a few times, but she had refused. Money was always scarce for both of them during the training, and afterwards, it was all over between them.

She tore open the silver wrapping paper on the cardboard box and slowly lifted the cover. The contents in it took her breath away. Nestled inside the tissue was a midnight blue outfit in crepe silk. She lifted the sequined halter neck top and the wrap-around skirt. It was perfect for her height and build. How had he guessed her size so accurately? The skirt even had a pocket that she could use to hide the gun. The outfit, Esha had to admit, was perfect for the evening and checked every item on her list of specifications for the dress.

The other box contained a pair of silver stilettos, the heels a good three inches high. Esha smiled. At least, here he had made a mistake. She would never wear high heels. They were a hindrance in case of an emergency.

⸺⸱≾⊹◉⊢≿⸱⊂⸺

There was no use procrastinating. Esha had heard Karisma's car driving in. Nikhil had honked twice. They had decided to use the regular protocol of two vehicles along with Vikram's bulletproof BMW.

Esha checked the gun in her pocket, took a deep breath, and descended the stairs. Nikhil stood there holding the passenger door open for her. Boy, he looked handsome. Wearing a grey tuxedo with his hair all sleeked, he was a treat to the feline eyes. He winked as he saw her and checked her out appreciatively. She smiled and slid into the plush front seat. Karisma, who was already seated at the back, greeted her.

"How did you guys meet? I mean Nick and you," Karisma asked.

"In Delhi, mutual acquaintances," Esha replied, glad that she didn't have to look at her.

"Where were you working prior to this job?"

"I was unemployed." For the first time, Esha prayed for the evening to get over soon. She wasn't disappointed when Vikram came out the next second and both men slid inside the car with Nikhil on the driver's seat and Vikram at the back.

The moment the door closed, the skin on her nape tingled. She was sure he was glaring at her. Making herself small, she shifted towards the window and thanked her stars that Karisma was hell-bent on monopolizing Vikram's attention.

The journey was uneventful as they reached the hotel. It was in the lift that that prickling sensation hit her again. Somehow she had ended up standing in front of Vikram. She was sure that if the term burning gaze held any truth, there'd be holes all over her back by now. His shoes touched her flat-soled sandals, but he didn't move back. The ride to the top floor was as draining as the marathon she used to run back at the training camp. Finally, when they reached the floor the restaurant was located on, Vikram and Karisma were escorted inside like celebrities. Nikhil and Esha followed them.

At the table, he didn't include her in the conversation with Nikhil and Karisma, refusing to even acknowledge her presence. Karisma threw smug glances at her, and Nikhil sat with a frown throughout.

She knew Vikram won't like that she didn't wear the outfit he had sent for her, but she never thought he would be so touchy about it. His complete indifference towards her pinched a little, but she sat observing other diners—her favorite pass time. After the second round of drinks, Vikram took Karisma to the dance floor.

"I don't know what's wrong with him," Nikhil broke into her thoughts.

"Why?"

"Don't tell me you haven't noticed. He has been flirting with you since the time you have come on board, ignoring Karisma. And now refuses to even look at you."

Esha smiled and shrugged.

"To hell with it. Let's dance, my Amazon." He pulled her out of her chair without even waiting for her affirmation. "So, how do you like it here?" He began the conversation after they were in the thick of the crowd, swaying with the music. There was no space for anything else.

"It's okay."

"You don't sound too enthusiastic."

"I sound enthusiastic only on the day my salary gets credited."

Throwing his head back, Nikhil laughed out and hugged her tight. "You are good for all of us, Xena. Life was monochromatic earlier and I feel so relieved with you around him. Jay is good, but he lacks... what do you call it... yes... 'spine'. He gets easily intimidated by Vikram."

Esha didn't correct him that the only difference between Jay and her was that she was able to hide her nerves. But she didn't want to talk about Vikram so she gave a perfunctory grin and left it at that. The song ended and they went back to their table. Vikram and Karisma were already seated with fresh drinks by their side.

As the band struck the chord for the next song, Vikram came near Esha and extended his hand for the dance. She had no choice but to get up. Boy, was she glad that she was dark and didn't visibly flush! But her whole body singed when he placed his arm around her waist and pulled her to him—close. Her hand on his chest resisted the close contact he had aimed for, but he didn't loosen his hold. Her gaze went from his third button to his eyes, which blankly studied her face. She dropped hers to look around at others over his shoulder.

"Now I'm not even fit for a glance, let alone an inane conversation."

Her eyes jerked back at him. What was wrong with him? He had been ignoring her the whole evening and now—

"Why didn't you wear that dress?"

"Can't accept a gift from you."

"Why not? Who bought this one? Nick?"

She frowned. "Why will he? I bought it."

He relaxed and smiled. "It would have looked good on you." He placed both her hands on his shoulder and slid his on her waist, pulling her even closer. "Wear it the next time we go out."

She stiffened, the air thick with their accelerated breaths.

"It's futile. Give up." His breath fanned her cheek as his thumb slid inside her top and caressed her back.

She was sure he could hear her heartbeats. Eyebrows furrowed, she glared at him. He grinned, causing her to almost give in.

"Go with the flow, we can't fight the chemistry between us. God knows I've tried—" His gaze flickered and hand stilled.

She turned to see what had captured his attention, thereby ending her torture.

Viraj stood at the bar, arguing with the bartender. Someone held his arm and another man tried to catch hold of his hand, in which he brandished a glass that was half-filled with pale yellow liquid.

Her gaze skimmed the hall and rested on their table where Karisma sat glaring at her drink. Catching Esha's glance, Nikhil smiled and winked. Thankfully the music ended and Vikram allowed her to step back.

"Meet me tomorrow at the gym, six a.m.," he said and escorted her back to the table.

Esha braced herself to get some flak from Karisma. She was sure that after that dance, she would have to face the jealous lover. Karisma was not like Urvi. She was a smart woman and couldn't be taken for granted.

"Where did you say you worked before joining Seth Industries, Ms. Sinha?" Karisma began the interrogation on the expected lines.

"Delhi."

"Where in Delhi? Which organization?"

"Why the sudden shop talk?" Nikhil intervened. "Let's dance. Karisma, come on. Do me the honor." He pulled Karisma's hand and shepherded the reluctant woman to the dance floor.

"Have something interesting other than that sparkling water," Vikram drawled. "Shall I—"

"I'm fine. Excuse me." Esha decided to spend the next few minutes in the washroom instead of sitting alone with him. Washrooms were so convenient at such times for a woman, she thought dryly.

"Running away?" Vikram said as soon as she stood up. He was an incorrigible, single track man. No wonder he succeeded in most of the things he did.

Somehow, she clung to her composure and made her way to the washroom. The mirror showed an image totally alien to hers. Her eyes looked tired and wane. Her skin had a moist sheen and her lips trembled. Nothing seemed in control. Taking a deep breath, she splashed cold water on her face and dabbed at the clinging droplets with a paper napkin. She hoped that the worse of the evening would be over once they moved to the dining area. With Karisma at the table, he would not dare to flirt with her.

She remained in the opulent, stone-cold room as long as it was decent, then stepped out only to find herself face-to-face with Karisma.

Eyebrows raised, Karisma stepped forward, causing Esha to step back into the washroom again.

"Since when has this been going on? And how can you two be so close, so soon? How did you manage to get into the inner coterie?"

"Perhaps you should direct this question at people who led me into that coterie?" Esha decided to be aggressive, a tactic that helped evade any honest answers, answers that she couldn't afford to give.

"You think you are pretty smart, don't you?" Karisma curled her lips. "I'll have you out of the company soon."

'*Get in the line.*' The thought almost made her smile. Esha sighed and stepped around Karisma to move out of the confined place and awkward situation. It was a relief that Karisma didn't pursue her.

Trouble had brewed at their table.

As she walked into the hall, she found Viraj in a heated exchange with Vikram. It was not an exchange in the real sense, because Vikram goaded Viraj simply by not participating in the discussion. Esha hurried towards their table when Nikhil stood up suddenly.

Esha was a table away when Viraj grabbed a bottle from a passing waiter's tray and smashed it on the table. He jabbed it at Vikram. Everything happened in microseconds. Alarmed, she rushed even as Nikhil tried to intervene, who was pushed back by Vikram. Viraj attacked Vikram again with the jagged edge of the bottle. But before Nikhil and the waiter could pry him away from the table, the damage had been done.

Droplets of blood from the wound rolled down Vikram's arm, while some fell on the table. The blow had done serious injury since he had taken off his jacket and rolled up the sleeves of his shirt after the dance.

Nikhil and the waiter pulled Viraj out of the hall.

"Are you all right?" she asked, checking his arm for any deep cuts or glass shards in the wound. The gash was long but she couldn't find anything to be alarmed about.

"Yeah..."

"It's not deep but I think we should get it examined. I have the doctor's number. I'll call him on the way."

The captain stood worried, apologizing profusely, muttering about calling a doctor, and asking them to step into his office.

"Let's go," Vikram said declining his help, but accepted the cotton gauge from the captain and pressed it on the wound. Esha tied his handkerchief over it. Nikhil was still not back. Picking up Vikram's jacket, she contacted Jay to meet them in the hotel exit and followed him out.

"Oh my God, what happened? Was that Viraj with Nick, I saw?" They remembered Karisma when she screeched, pulling at Vikram's arm. "Hell, did he do that? We should call the police. Do you need stitches?"

"Maybe. But it's nothing to worry about," Esha said.

"How do you know? Move aside. He needs a doctor. You'll definitely need stitches. Look at the amount of blood!"

"Oh, for God's sake stop the theatrics. It's nothing," Vikram snapped as they entered the elevators.

But that didn't stop Karisma from overreacting and showing how much she cared. She dialed Vikram's mother and sister's numbers and broadcasted the news.

Esha was in touch with Nikhil, who followed them in the second car after handing over a much stoned Viraj under the care of his driver.

The doctor was already there when they arrived home. Nikhil asked Karisma if she wanted a drop home. She gave him a stony look and didn't leave Vikram's side. Once assured that Vikram and the premises were secured, Esha retired for the night. There was no point in hovering in the living room since his mother and sister had arrived too.

What an evening, Esha thought when she made it back to her room. She picked up the dossier on Viraj and re-read the key summary points she had jotted down. This was the second time he had attacked Vikram.

Viraj had quite a few points against him but she hadn't pegged him to be a killer or hire someone for the same. Although she couldn't deny that he did have a motive—a very strong motive. He would get his freedom if Vikram was not in the picture. But no one, who wanted someone murdered, would gather so many witnesses to his hatred. Even if he was taking someone's help, even if he hired someone, he wouldn't reveal his intentions the way he did tonight.

Though Viraj wasn't off her list of suspects, Esha hadn't considered him a serious threat either. But after tonight's episode, she knew he had to be put somewhere on the top of her list. She added her thoughts in his file in the margins.

October 13th

He meticulously lifted the hair on the trap door and went down the stairs. Cleaning himself, he sat in front of Kaali Maa's idol and began the blood ritual.

And the monologue began.

After each of his unsuccessful attempts, Vikram's aide, that Nikhil, had tightened and changed the security and the protocols. He wasn't able to break anything or anyone. All the guards were well-paid and firmly under Nikhil's control. He was running out of options.

However, Viraj's temper and his violent outburst, the night of the dinner, had given him the fodder to think from another perspective. Could this be another red herring that could give him the required cover for another attempt?

'Could this be a sign from you Maa?'

He looked up into the eyes of the ferocious, unmoving statue, but couldn't look into her eyes for more than two seconds. Her austere persona terrified yet consumed him. He focused his gaze at the devil crushed under her feet, wishing he could crush the Seths like that. He silently pleaded to Maa to talk to him, to guide him, but she remained silent.

He suddenly remembered that he should be meditating and picked up the rudraksh string. He shook off his thoughts about his enemies and concentrated on the rituals that would make his mother happy.

"Om Krim Kaaliaaye Namah!" he chanted as he sifted a bead through his fingers. The itch to kill the bastard became

stronger with each rudraksh bead that passed through his fingers.

He concentrated on the light from the lamp filtering through his eyelid and pictured his maker on the canvas of his mind. Sara's face appeared instead. Tears flowing down her cheeks, pleading to take revenge on her behalf. He had vowed to avenge her honor and inflict wounds on the enemy as no one else could, but the satisfaction had eluded him. The justified hate had consumed most of his life. Maa was still to grant him their wish. What had gone wrong in his devotion and penance, he often wondered

In the materialistic world, money played a significant role too. In fact, it was a game changer. Everything needed money, which they had in plenty and he didn't have any. No one was supposed to prosper like the way they had, while his Sara had suffered.

He had to succeed. Sara had entrusted this responsibility on him. To destroy them. To avenge her. To inflict upon them the kind of grief no one had ever experienced.

His fingers touched the soft silk thread that indicated that he had come to the end of the necklace. He realized, however, that he had stopped chanting the mantra somewhere in between. Lost in his thoughts when did he stop the chanting? This had never happened! His eyes flew up to Maa. Her gaze now had anger mixed with pity. His courage sank to the pit of his stomach.

The mobile rang. The ring stopped after five seconds. He connected using one of the unregistered SIMs.

"Mahajan has spoken to someone at the car parking in Delhi and that man has given him the name of the girl."

"Is it so?" he asked.

"*Yes.*"

He stood silent, contemplating the repercussions.

"*Aren't you bothered?*"

"*That has been taken care of.*" *He disconnected the call.*

For once he felt ahead in the game, but the next moment it came to him that the years of preparation for the Delhi attack had all gone down the drain. It had taken him six months of recce to zero on Debbie because she was in the flesh trade and yet secretive and emotional. Then another three months were wasted to befriend and fool her to do his bidding. It had taken him immense control to mask his disgust when he had been with her. All that sacrifice and torture had gone down the drain.

Noise from one of the speakers from the room above alerted him.

Sara was awake.

⸻ ❖ ⸻

SETHS' RESIDENCE, MUMBAI
13TH OCTOBER, 7:00 AM

Esha was ready by seven and entered the bungalow through the kitchen. Kishore *dada* was busy arranging a breakfast tray. "They are on the terrace."

Looking at the number of plates in the sink, it seemed like Vikram's mother, his sister, and Karisma had stayed the night.

"Don't bother, I'll have my breakfast here in the kitchen."

She didn't go to meet Nikhil or Vikram. There was no need. With all his well-wishers around him, her presence would be perceived as awkward, given that it was also a Sunday. She was just an employee after all and a temporary one at that.

After having her breakfast, Esha went back to her apartment but a strange restlessness stuck to her soul and refused to subside.

An hour later, she saw Karisma drive off. A constant stream of visitors kept arriving and leaving. Esha picked up the unfinished novel and tried to immerse herself in the story, but nothing helped. Finally, she took off to see Mumbai city.

She roamed around, taking a local train or an auto, and finally arrived at Marine Drive after three hours of aimless wandering in the streets of the financial capital of the country.

The sea looked calm and quiet, with tides gently lapping against the man-made stone boulders. Esha felt as lonely as the sea. Surrounded by everyone, yet no one for a real companion. Never had her solitude been so pronounced. After that obligatory call home that she had arrived safely, she had not spoken to her mother. Her younger sister had called once for money, which she had transferred that same day. No one called her without any need. If she died, no one would come to know for days. For this very reason, she had kept specific instructions in a sealed envelope in her personal effects so that they won't be missed.

As she took in the sea whirling on the shores, and nearby sites, a familiar figure interrupted her musings. A cold wave prickled the hair on her nape, which reminded her of the visit to Jindal's office.

Koel stood on the other side of the road with a man on a motorcycle, who looked like the guard she had seen in Jindal's office. The one in the uniform at the gate. Though he wasn't wearing the uniform today, he looked like the same person. Esha wasn't sure. If he was the same person why was Koel talking to him? Koel with her lofty standards meeting a mere guard, that too from Jindal's office.

The man handed Koel a packet, then drove off. Nikhil had to be informed about this.

Her phone pinged pulling her out of the troubling thoughts. 'Be there at dinner. Tonight.' Vikram had ordered.

Instead of feeling offended at the high-handed tone of the message, she found herself smiling. There was someone who wanted her, even if it was for all the wrong reasons. She chuckled at the thought. Her loneliness vanished without a trace. If nothing else, she would have this memory of the day when she was pitying herself and one message from the mighty Vikramaditya Seth Jr., the most influential 'Indian of the Year' had lifted her spirits. Goddamn! What could be more pathetic than that, Major Esha Sinha? She snorted and hailed a cab.

⸻⬦⬦⸻

The whiff of cigarette assailed her the moment she entered the dining room. The whole room was shrouded in darkness except the table that had a candelabra holding five huge candles sitting at one end of the table. To her acute panic, there were only two covers on the table. Where was Nikhil? She had expected him to act as a much-needed buffer.

"You look as fetching in a skirt as in a pair of jeans." The voice came from somewhere near the buffet table to her right. Vikram stood there holding a bottle. "I've decided that we'll have some red wine." He shook a finger when she opened her mouth. "No, don't object. I have to make up for yesterday. Viraj ruined everything last night. I owe you a nice relaxing dinner." His left arm was bandaged and in a sling and he used only his right hand.

"You don't owe me anything. And why are you using a sling?" Esha frowned. As far as she could see, there was no damage to the bone last night.

"You don't know?" An eyebrow went up. "You have been so callous with me, Major. Taking off without even bothering to ask about my injury. It's quite serious." He tilted the bottle towards her. "Please do me the honor of opening this."

"There was no damage to the bone last night. I had examined it." She deftly uncorked the bottle and smelled it. The wine was a deep red and perfect. "Would you like to taste it or shall I pour?"

He smiled and shook his head. "I love the way you work. Precisely, with minimum fuss. Let me take it from here." He moved towards the dining table where the wine glasses were kept, along with the three-course meal on the warmer at the center. Having missed her lunch, Esha suddenly realized that she was quite hungry.

"I'll not drink."

"Why not?"

"I'm not in the habit of drinking with my employer."

He took a deep breath. "For a while can you forget that I'm your employer? Forget everything. Please. Just remember that we are two attractive, single people having the hots for each other." He caught hold of her glance and somehow she couldn't look away.

Her lips twitched at his words. It was funny to hear someone praising themselves so honestly and earnestly. It took some effort to control her smile.

Watching her all the time, he took a sip and brought their glasses to the dining table.

"What should I do to make you relax and smile?" He lifted his spoon. "And don't tell me you are a serious person. I have seen you with Nick."

"Talking about Nick, I have to tell him to keep an eye on Koel and re-look at the guards who are with Jindal's security."

"Sure. Do that. But I won't get distracted by shop-talk today. You haven't answered my question."

Her phone rang just then. It was an unknown number. She swiped with her finger to answer the call but her finger slipped and the phone went on to speaker mode.

"Hello..."

"Esha, I can't live like this." The familiar voice was slurred and came over the din of high bass music.

"Samar?" She glanced at Vikram. He was clearly miffed at the interruption.

"Esha, I have to see you... I need you..." She hurriedly kept the spoon down and switched off the speaker mode.

Excusing herself with a shrug, she moved to the window at the far end of the room. "Where are you?"

"Esha, can you imagine I'm at my bachelors' party? I can't go through this... I don't love her. I love you."

"Samar, it's been two years," she hissed.

"Yes, I know. But I can't commit to her. I don't feel anything for her."

"This is ridiculous. You are drunk. Everything will be all right in the morning."

"Esha, please."

"I have moved on, Samar and you should too." Esha disconnected the call. She could have been sympathetic but it would have made him more persistent. For all she knew, he might not even remember he had called in the morning. It was for the best. Taking a deep calming breath, she turned from the window and found Vikram watching her with keen interest.

"Another broken heart that you have left somewhere?"

She took another deep breath and concentrated on the soup. "Where is Kishore *dada*?"

He shifted her wine glass towards her bowl. Feeling that she would need the alcohol to get through the evening, she took a sip and served the fish-finger cutlets on both their plates.

"Who was he? Sounded desperate."

"Do we have to do this?" She lifted her eyes at him and caught him off guard. He wasn't expecting a direct approach. She had had enough and could never play blind.

"What?"

"This flirting and all..." She waved her spoon around.

"Deny that you aren't attracted to me."

"I won't. Yes, I am attracted to you."

His eyes fluttered at the unexpected confession, but he recovered in a split second and smiled. "And I am to you."

Her heart skipped a beat. "So? That doesn't mean we need to give in to all our whims."

"Why not? As long as we aren't hurting others or breaking any rules, I don't see why we should hold back."

"I'll be breaking a rule."

"Which rule?"

"Mine. I don't get involved with my... er..."

"Package?"

She shook her head. "I was about to say, employer. Keeping you safe is my responsibility and these things... the emotions, they distract. We are talking about a life here... There are too many variables and we shouldn't add another one to the equation. This is serious."

Vikram looked at her for a long moment then nodded. "Now that you have put it like this, it makes sense."

She remained silent.

"So what do we do about this attraction?" he asked.

"We don't give it any importance."

"Pretend that it doesn't exist?"

"Yes."

"I think it is a bad idea, but we'll play by your rules Major. Let's see where this takes us."

Astounded, she watched him serve the salad. She had never thought it would be so easy. Never thought he would be so reasonable.

It took Esha a few minutes to get over her surprise as he continued to tell her about his family—things mainly related to security and a few mishaps that had happened due to a lapse in the security or their own mistakes. Some of these accounts were hilarious, while some scared her.

The rest of the meal was completed in total truce. The undercurrents were there every time their eyes met or hands touched, but they were not at the forefront anymore. Esha admitted to herself that he could be a pleasant man to talk to if he chose to be.

Later she sent a message on her misgiving about Koel and the guard she saw in the afternoon to Nikhil. He answered back immediately saying he would put her under surveillance in an hour.

⸻❖⸻

KEM MORGUE, MUMBAI
13TH OCTOBER, 7:30 PM

"This way, sir." The policeman led Nikhil to a small room off the main morgue. "The body was found today on the beach, washed by the morning tide. The rot is yet to set, but it is bloated. Not a pretty sight," he warned and pulled the sheet from a body laid on a stretcher.

An unexpected wave of sympathy overwhelmed Nikhil as he lay his eyes on the young girl. She had been tortured brutally before her life was taken. The open wounds and the burn marks told the story that her last hours had been horrific. A life snuffed out just for helping and trusting a wrong man.

"How do you know she is Debbie?"

"Her friend from Kamathipura has identified her by a birthmark and a gold ring."

"So he didn't take the ring. Do you have the friend's name and contact details?"

"Yes, sir."

"Ask her to see me in my office, immediately."

"Yes, sir."

October 14th

The girl looked totally out of place in his plush office. Nikhil studied her from the one-way glass door. It had taken his team two precious days to locate her. Wearing a pair of blue jeans and a skimpy pink top, she looked not more than nineteen years of age. She looked nervous, yet stood confidently in the lobby. He opened the door and called her in.

"Sit down," he ordered.

She obliged.

"How long have you known Debbie?"

"You call me to talk about Debbie?" She pouted. "I tell everything to thee police. I thot—"

"Shut up." He banged the table.

Startled, she sat back looking at him with large moist eyes.

"I ask questions and you give answers, that's it."

She looked positively agitated after a few seconds of stunned silence.

"What's the problem?"

"I thot I get some work here, big people, big money."

"What kind of work do you do?"

To his irritation, she gave him a coy smile and said, "I do naughty, naughty things to men and they give money. Loads of money."

At first, Nikhil thought she said something in *Marathi* but the next second it hit him that she was talking about sexual favors.

"I'll give you money to give me honest answers to my questions."

"How much?"

He smiled. She was a tough one. "Depends on your answers. You have to make me happy. Honest the answer, more the money."

"How you know I give honest answer?"

"I'll know."

"Okay." Nodding her head, she got comfortable in the chair and said, "Let's play."

He almost laughed at the child-woman.

"How do you know Debbie?"

"She and I doubled up sometime. She an honest girl."

"Doubled up?"

"You never doubled up?" Before he could reply, she leaned forward and whispered. "Some people like sandwich kind. Much fun with two girls, not much when there two mans. They get rough sometime." She wrinkled her nose.

Gosh, who was he dealing with?

"So, she was your friend?"

"Yes."

"Did you know who all she met in the last two-three weeks? Anyone new?"

"She meet many mans."

"I mean anyone who came frequently, more than once? Someone who was friendly?"

"Yes. There was a man who loved Debbie, she said. She tell me, he loved her not her body. Asked her to leave everything because he has lots of money."

"What was his name?"

"Lakshman"

So she had given him a name, but it meant nothing. "Have you seen him?"

"No." She shook her head, then immediately nodded. "Yes, once actually. Not like face to face, but in the window pane. He very secretive. Say from good family, but love Debbie."

"Okay, can you describe him?"

"*Gora*, like Nepali peoples. Saw his nose, very nice, straight nose. Always wore full-sleeve checked shirt."

"Is that all?" He asked incredulously.

"Yes... they both very secretive." She nodded.

God! Either she was a simpleton or a consummate liar. Nikhil was leaning towards the former. "Okay, so can you sit with an artist and help him get a sketch?"

She nodded. "I honest. My money."

He took out a wad of five-hundred-rupee notes and tossed it on the table. She shrieked in delight and pounced on the bundle.

Nikhil dialed the number of the artist while the girl counted the notes.

⊸⊷⊶⊷⊶⊷⊶⊶

VERSOVA, MUMBAI
14TH OCTOBER, 7:30 PM

Aaryan rushed towards Vikram the moment he entered his sister's apartment. It was Aaryan's birthday. The kids had left and now the celebrations continued with only close family members.

"Where is my gift, Vikram?"

"Gift, what gift?" Vikram teased the little bundle of energy. But the smile vanished as he spotted Urvi's mother deep in conversation with his own on one of the sofas. He cringed at the thought of meeting Urvi, but didn't spot her in the hall. He couldn't understand his mother's affection towards Urvi and persistence to push them towards a reconciliation. She seemed to value the institution of marriage more than her son's happiness. More than her mother's motivations, he wondered at his own wisdom in marrying Urvi. He had been dazzled by her on-screen persona when he had come back from the US and had gone along with his mother's enthusiasm of seeing her son married to her childhood friend's daughter.

"Gift! It's my birthday, Vikram!" Aaryan tugged at his trousers.

"Aaryan, he is your *mama!*" *daija* said from the dining area.

"No, he is my buddy, and one calls their friend by their name. It's cool. Isn't it Vikram?" Aaryan said.

"Yes, totally." Vikram ruffled his hair. "Where are your other buddies?"

"Vikram, you are spoiling him," Vandana shouted from the kitchen. "Aaryan be careful about *mama's* arm."

"They are gone, now the party is for big people." Aaryan twitched his nose answering Vikram. "Now it is a boring adult party, but we'll have fun. Won't we?"

Vikram chuckled at the disdain the little one showed to the adults. His mother muttered something about lack of manners and adult supervision.

"Where is my gift?"

"It's on its way. Have patience, young man. It's a surprise!" Vikram said.

"I don't like surprises." Aaryan pouted.

"Don't make faces like that! It's not fitting for a prince like you," *daija* said, placing the smaller, eggless cake at the center of the table, which was for the family.

"Am I really a prince, grandma?"

"No, I think *daija* said that... because you know... since you are such a cute little boy."

"No, I'm a prince. And mom is a queen."

"And papa is a king, right?" Meera Seth chuckled.

"No, he is an ogre."

The silence that filled the hall had frozen the entire adult population, which meant everyone other than Aaryan. "What is an ogre, Vikram?"

"Who told you that?" Vandana asked keeping an amused expression on her face.

"*Daija* said that to you when she thought I was sleeping," Aaryan revealed with a sheepish smile.

Luckily Jay arrived with the gift that Vikram had ordered. Aaryan's enthusiasm distracted them from the awkward moment but the underlying tension amongst the adults remained throughout dinner. Their mother complained about *daija's* influence over Aaryan and Vandana giving too much leeway to *daija,* which made Vandana irritable.

Urvi's mother kept whispering into his mother's ears whenever she thought people were not looking at them, but everyone knew. *Daija* tried to make herself inconspicuous by remaining in the kitchen the entire evening. The fact that Jindal arrived after the dinner was over and Aaryan was put to bed, added to their angst.

Thank god, his mother had to leave for the airport else she would have accompanied Vikram back home and would have complained throughout the way.

October 15th

Esha scanned the hall once again. The master of ceremony was closing the event with the last speech. Some of the guests were moving towards the bar area.

She roamed around, casually sipping the ice-water while keeping Vikram in sight. He stood talking to an elegant woman in a sari. Esha stiffened as she spied the woman's hand on his arm. He listened to her with undivided focus, a part of his personality. With extreme effort, she peeled her gaze off him and scanned the hall, mentally noting the exits, observing people, and relaying any important information to Nikhil, who was downstairs, over her phone. Her glance went to Vikram again. She sighed. He had moved to another group. Her jealous state of heart was not good for the grave responsibility she had been given, Esha reminded herself.

Her senses went into an all alert, as she saw a burly man standing close to him. A little too close. Her hand went to her pocket and she took a step forward. The man moved and she relaxed. Nikhil, who had come to the hall by now, stood in the opposite corner talking to a tall, handsome man she had never seen before. Every now and then one of them would glance at Vikram.

She glanced at the master of ceremony and spotted Urvi with her. Her presence at a corporate event surprised Esha. Urvi's hands flew all over as she spoke, her face animated. They both laughed and glanced at Vikram. It seemed he was the center of attention for not only Esha but for everyone present in that room. And then she noticed Karisma entering the hall.

What a bizarre world they lived in? Existing together, in the same social circles, seeing each other, vying for the same man's attention, fanning his ego. Each driven by their wants and desires. Urvi, Esha knew, wanted his money. What did Karisma want? She was jealous about Esha the other day. But was it just her ego or did she have genuine feelings for him?

Wouldn't it be demeaning meeting each other and pretending to be friendly in light of their relationships? Esha could never dream to be in the same social circles as Samar. The thought reminded her again how different her world was compared to theirs.

⚯

'The whole visit was a waste,' Vikram thought.

The CNBC event hadn't lived up to his expectations that year. The organizers were more concerned about the TRP instead of substance. Lost in his thought, he walked behind Nikhil as they exited the building. Esha and two of the guards were behind them.

"Why is the car not here?" Nikhil frowned and stepped forward. "Where the hell is Jay?"

"What about the other car?" Esha asked, moving forward, making Vikram come to an abrupt halt as he collided with her.

Another visitor stepped down on the last step as the valet brought his car.

"Nick, something's not right. Someone's watching us. I can feel it. Check out the car at 2 o'clock."

When she stepped right in front covering him, Vikram's brain caught the urgency in her voice.

"The windows are dark and one of them is slightly open. No, someone up, on the roof... ah." She jerked against Vikram as her right hand went to her left shoulder.

The briefcase slipped from Vikram's grip as his arms went around her. She faltered as he supported her. Then he heard the familiar whistling sound and felt her jerk again and this time she went limp against him. Nikhil shouted. The two guards converged on him.

Darkness of fear swam in front of Vikram's eyes as her body went heavy in a dead faint. He staggered with the thrust of her weight and sat back supporting her. "Esha!" his own voice echoed in his ears.

"Nick!" Vikram shouted, as Nikhil took out his gun and ran towards the traffic exposing himself. The cars screeched. There was no way he could help Nikhil with Esha lying dead in his arms. His shirt stuck to his skin and he touched the moist patch on his chest and looked at the maroon-red blood on his fingers.

⊰•≼◆≽•⊱

Esha wanted to go somewhere. She opened her eyes but a sharp pain made her close her eyes again.

A car screeched.

Trying to reach out to someone, she willed her eyes to open but could not against the bright blinding sun shining in her eyes. Breathing brought excruciating pain around her chest. She wanted something that she couldn't remember and became restless. Fighting the pain, she thrashed against the hands holding and poking at her. Her hands entangled into something that felt like a wire, she jerked away from it. Her head went here and there, trying to locate something, someone, whom, she wasn't sure...

"She's coming around..."

Someone spoke on her right, and then Vikram called out her name. A hand held hers in a firm grip. A familiar scent hit her nose. The white light around her faded a bit and she could make out a figure frowning at her. He was all right. He was breathing. She exhaled, but couldn't understand who was holding her though. She stopped thrashing as the pain to her shoulder registered and took deep breaths. It felt her left side had been severed. She tried to hold her shoulder with her right hand, but couldn't feel her fingers. A second later, as her fingers encountered something hot and sticky, there was complete oblivion.

———⟐⟐⟐———

SUBURBS, MUMBAI
15TH OCTOBER, 7:30 PM

He lifted the trapdoor and stepped down into the stairwell. Rage burning strong in his chest, he wanted to smash everything to smithereens. More than that, he wanted to put the barrel against his temple and pull the trigger.

Luck. That was the only thing that came to his mind. The bastard was damn lucky!

How could he have known that the secretary would step in front of him at the last moment? A woman! A woman again. Damn, damn, damn!

Seth, it seemed, had got nine lives.

He loaded the .45, his favorite weapon and touched the muzzle of the gun to his temple.

His phone rang with the customary two rings, then became silent. The sound doused away the fire in his mind and he was left panting under the shroud of his anger. The phone beckoned him and he picked up a random SIM and inserted it in a random phone set.

"Hello."

The silence at the other end brought another wave of disappointment.

"Never mind." The voice on the other side finally spoke.

"I need money for the next round. This time, there will be no expenses spared."

"Yes, I know. I have arranged for it, the usual way. You can pick it from the locker. Is the man in the taxi silenced?"

"Yes."

"Are you okay?"

He wasn't. He was bruised all over and a shard of glass had pierced his thigh when he was scaling the boundary wall of the building. "I'm fine," he lied.

The line went dead. Time was up.

Hell!

When will you stop testing me, Maa? How many failures can your devotee take? I have sacrificed my life to you and this mission. I have sacrificed everything—my family, my heart, and my soul. Why is my sacrifice not enough? What else do you need?

His grip on the gun tightened again. He wanted to go to Seths' residence and gun Jr. down then and there. So many times, he had wanted to poison him, but after doing that no one could have escaped, such was the security net laid down by Nikhil.

The sonofabitch was on his trail like a bloodthirsty nagin, still sniffing around Debbie's rooms and that stupid friend of hers.

What if someone else had seen his face? He had been extremely careful, but there could always be someone lurking in the corners, keeping an eye on everything and everyone. There was no dearth of people fishing for information to sell. The risks were mounting and the end was nowhere near.

No, no, no, he shouldn't panic. He should keep his cool.

Probably he needed another distraction to free his mind from the depressing chain of thoughts. He got up, opened his laptop, and searched the Internet.

October 16th

Esha tried to open her eyes but her eyelids seemed to be glued together. A machine beeped at regular intervals placed somewhere to her left. Opening her eyes was an effort, so she didn't bother. A shadow moved in the periphery of her vision then disappeared. She heard the door close, then silence reigned in the room. She drifted off to sleep again.

The next time Esha woke up, she could open her eyes. The room looked surreal. Every horizontal surface in the room had a bouquet on it. A nurse stood near a chest of drawers with her face in the blooms.

"Aren't we spoilt?" she said sheepishly when she turned to find Esha's gaze on her. "Look at all the flowers! You are one lucky woman. He adores you." She wheeled in the breakfast trolley near the bed and cranked up her bed.

Esha frowned.

Though she wanted to be left alone, she had many questions and wanted detailed information, so she tolerated the nurse fussing around her.

Two cars had crashed on the curb when Nikhil ran on the road, but no one else was hurt. It would take at least two weeks for her wound to heal, she was told. The flowers, all of them, were sent by Vikram or his family, and the best room had been arranged by his orders. The nurse chattered away cheerfully going about her chores, not mentioning anything else about the incident.

Esha was given her medicines, a sponge bath, and her hair was brushed. All the things were brand new and classy, brought in by Seth sir himself, she was informed. It amused Esha to know that she was under security with two guards stationed in front of her room 24 X 7.

"Can you get me a newspaper?"

"No, we are not allowed newspapers here. Doctor's order."

Someone knocked. The nurse opened the door to find Mrs. Seth standing with her secretary close behind. Hesitant but smiling tentatively, Mrs. Seth entered the room. It seemed she had aged by years in a couple of days. The secretary handed a basket of fruits to the nurse.

"How are you? Are the doctor and staff treating you well?"

"Yes, thank you, Mrs. Seth. You shouldn't have bothered."

"Of course, I had to come. I... I don't know how to thank you. You have been so brave. He would have died, if—" She held Esha's hand and squeezed it. "The threat has always been there, for us, his father, for him... but two attacks in a month..."

"Nick will find out who is behind this. You needn't worry."

She smiled. "Yes... er... The doctor told me about your injury. Luckily, none of the bullets touched your bone. If you want we can go for plastic surgery as well.

Then there would be no scar, and you'll be able to wear sleeveless dresses."

'Dress? Sleeveless? What was she talking about?'

"No... no, that won't be necessary."

Mrs. Seth sighed. "Vikram tells me that you have no one to go to at the moment. I have come to invite you to Alibaug for the coming weekend. We have a pre-Diwali bash there every year. Some traditions have to be followed, no matter what. They keep us anchored. It will be a good break for you too. I'll be happy if you decide to join us."

"Thanks a lot." Esha smiled. Goddamn! She was sure he must have ordered his mother to invite her. She then wondered about the man himself. Was he so busy that he couldn't find time to visit her?

"Okay then. The doctor said not to tire you too much. Esha, our entire family will be indebted to you forever."

Esha inept at taking compliments and following social etiquettes, smiled and nodded.

"Nick is waiting to meet you too. Please rest and call me or Reema if you want anything." Mrs. Seth nodded at her secretary. "And I mean anything. God bless." She smiled and left the room.

"So how is my Xena?" Nikhil entered immediately after Mrs. Seth went out. Sitting beside her on the bed, he picked up a grape from the basket.

"Hey, they are for me."

"Is that so?" He picked up another and took it to her lips.

"It's not washed!"

"Xenas of the world do not eat washed fruits." He rubbed the grape on his trousers and forced it into her mouth, then the laughter faded away from his eyes. "You saved him, Major."

"Ah, not you too!"

"Yes, you did. It was your shoulder or his heart."

"Get over it." Embarrassed, Esha changed the subject. "Any clue?"

"Nope. We thought someone in the car took a shot, but it was not the vehicle. He was high up on the top floor of the three-story building across the road. The weapon has been abandoned again. Customized, like in Delhi. The guy knows his guns. Have to give him that. No fingerprints, not a bloody strand of hair. He comes well-prepared. Has loads of money too."

Nikhil brought her up to speed about the entire private investigation that his friend and renowned investigator Uday was conducting and the status so far. The likely people who could identify the killer were not many and the one who could, had been eliminated.

"He is a pro. A steady shooter, level headed," she said, glad that Nikhil trusted her now. Though she had kept her sentiments hidden, it frustrated her when she didn't have the complete picture. "Both times, the shots didn't vary much as far as the distance is concerned. Ask me." She smiled glancing at her bandaged shoulder. "Search for someone with an army background."

"Yeah, we are doing exactly that. I'll keep you posted."

The nurse coughed somewhere from the corner of the room indicating that visiting time was up.

He stood up. "You take care. I want to see you soon, lying above me."

"Ha, ha." She snorted.

He grinned, winked at the nurse who turned red, and left the room picking a bunch of grapes from the basket.

October 18th

Bullets rained everywhere. Someone ran with her—a friend. She could hear the panting but couldn't see anyone. They had nowhere to go in the dense fog surrounding the city. It was the end that was certain. Where was he? She couldn't see him. Was he safe? She had to find him. His safety was the only thought that plagued her, as she ran through the maze of buildings. The concrete structures with no doors or windows were both high as well as low, but there was no respite. Whosoever wanted them dead was going to succeed. He was going to win! A bullet whizzed past, narrowly missing her head.

She sat gasping for air and then doubled up as her brain registered the pain in her shoulder. Someone enveloped her in a bear hug. She struggled against the light embrace. "Let go... let me go... let me..."

"Esha, hush. You are safe." Vikram held her, murmuring something incoherent and soothing. Even in the haze of pain, she knew it was him—the subtle whiff of his customized cologne was unmistakable. When the spasm of pain eased and her breathing returned to normal, he loosened his hold and gently rested his chin on her forehead.

"What are you doing here?" she asked when she was sure that she would not sound breathless.

"Visiting you. During the nights... past few days. Couldn't come during the day."

Goddamn! She closed her eyes.

"Should I call the nurse? They can give you something for the pain."

She shook her head. "No, I can't think with all those meds running in my blood."

His lips touched her temple. "You are not supposed to think. You are supposed to rest."

"Oh God. You shouldn't be here! Where is Nick? Guards!" She pushed at his arms, looking around frantically.

"Shh... shh... relax, they are all out there, I wanted to see you... to just look at you." He caressed her cheek, his eyes all tender, his breath on her face making her insides squirm and melt. "I have always wondered about the motivation behind Nikhil's manic dedication to me after that accident in the mountains. But now... now I think I understand him. It is like a life-long debt, one that can never be repaid."

Pushing him away, Esha lay back on the bed to escape the need to hug him back, to feel him. "I never thought you would be the philosophical kind."

Vikram chuckled. "You can quit acting like a distant employee. Do you want me to call any of your family members?" He held her hand and made circles on her skin with his thumb.

"No," she blurted, then realized the need to defend her statement. "I don't want to blow my cover. It's not serious. I don't want to worry them unnecessarily."

He nodded, looking so handsome and alive that her pain and the ordeal lost its relevance. She suppressed an urge to straighten her hair. Why should she worry about how she looked? *'Esha Sinha, you are in a serious mess'.*

"What's the day today... time...?" she asked to cover her bare emotions.

"It's Monday, midnight. Three days since you were brought here." He continued to look at her in the same endearing way as if she was God and his only love rolled into one.

"Now that you have seen that I'm alive and breathing, I think you should go. It's quite late." She tried not to squirm under his gaze.

"Why? Am I making you uncomfortable?" He lifted her hand and kissed her wrist.

"I don't want others to be out of bed on my account." She closed her eyes and tried not to respond to his touch.

"Others... huh?" He chuckled shaking his head. "You go off to sleep, don't worry about the others."

"Oh, for God's sake it's just a flesh wound. You are making it sound like I have woken up from my death bed."

"Well, it appeared like that, that evening. Do you have any idea how I felt when I saw your blood on my shirt?" His grasp on her hand tightened. "I can't even explain what I went through when you collapsed in my arms, Esha. I went berserk when you went limp... fu—" He cursed under his breath as his phone rang. "Yeah... yeah. I'm coming."

Disconnecting the call, he sighed. "I have to go to Singapore for a few days, then to the US. Just hang on, okay. We'll talk when I'm back."

"You are going abroad? Who is going with you?" She scowled.

Vikram smiled. "Don't worry, this time I have accepted the Z-plus security from the government. You take care of yourself. I want you up and about when I am back." He gave her a light peck at the corner of her lips and left, making the room cold and colorless.

⸺❖⸺

SUBURBS, MUMBAI
18TH OCTOBER, 6:30 PM

Sitting in his room, *he watched the footage of the shooting outside the CNBC event for the nth time. Someone had recorded the video and he had downloaded it immediately before the Seths could put a media gag on the clip. His whole focus was on the PA who had stepped forward in the nick of time. She had spoken something rapidly, spurring Nikhil into action. How could she be so alert? So vigilant?*

Alert like a bodyguard!

His hands started trembling. He replayed the clip and his hunch became a reality. She definitely had that smart, crisp demeanor about her—the aura of someone who had gone through a rigorous physical regime.

The thought brought a wave of panic and impotency. Who was she? When was she recruited? Was she undercover? He'd have to get more information on her. How did she skip his radar!

Damn! Damn!

⸺❖⸺

October 19th

Uday's reports were on Nikhil's desk that morning when he reached office. With Esha in the hospital, he had had to be with Vikram all the time.

He had asked Uday to give him a report on people who had been fired from the army or had taken voluntary retirement and were in the age bracket of twenty-eight to fifty. Uday had segregated the reports based on who had been fired from the army and the ones who had taken voluntary retirement.

Nikhil needed someone to help him to zero down the bastard—someone whom he could trust to sift through the thick reports with a cool head. Esha was his best bet since she couldn't be on the field anyway till she was recuperating, but he'd have to discuss the situation with Vikram, who didn't want her under any stress at all. But knowing Esha, Nikhil was sure she would love to crack the puzzle. She had earned the right to be involved in all the details.

"The motherfucker is in Mumbai." Vikram stormed into his office. "Nick, who had the means to buy the parts of a gun and the skills to assemble it? Whoever he is, he shouldn't be able to hide from us."

"Don't worry, a contact has been made with someone in the underbelly of Mumbai."

"I want to personally find him and beat him to pulp." Vikram paced the length of the room.

"Vikram—" Frowning, Nikhil watched him agitated and worried for the first time in so many years.

"I can't rest till he is caught. I'm worried about mom and *di* too. I wish I can get involved in the investigations." He raked his hair with his fingers. "I wish there was someone to handle the business so that I can play an active role in hunting the bastard down. And I don't want to go and leave her here. Nick, I—"

"Relax. Just relax. I'm here." Nikhil stood up knowing who he referred to. "Everyone is under our radar and protection. Have I ever let you down? Uday and I are on top of this, we are definitely going to find some weakness in his armor." Nikhil somehow pacified him and took him to the airport.

Later in the evening, Nikhil contacted the artist who was working with child-hooker.

"Has she given anything?" Nikhil asked.

"No sir, I'm still working with her." The artist sounded harassed and tired. "She is so fickle minded, keeps changing and adding her own imagination, and keeps propositioning me. I'm not too hopeful."

"Okay."

"Though I don't think she is lying."

"Yeah, right. Arrange for another session, if nothing comes out, it's okay. Give her the money and let her go."

The trail was getting cold. The arms-dealer lead had to be relentlessly pursued. What can be done to trap him? Nikhil's hands fisted and his eyes took on a steely glint as an idea began to sprout and slowly take shape. He picked up his phone and dialed a number.

October 28th

Esha came out of the bathroom with only a towel around her and found Nikhil lounging in the easy chair in her room. She pursed her lips and arranged the towel more securely around her torso.

"Oh, sorry!" Nikhil said without any remorse and continued to sit, watching her with his habitual relaxed smile.

She sighed. "Why did I expect you to look away? There is a knocker on the door I believe."

"The door was not locked, Xena."

"So—"

The door opened again.

"Esha, how are—" Vikram stopped short as he took in the scene.

He was back!

Esha's face went warm at the sight of him. "Fine come on in, we are having an orgy out here. What do you guys have against knocking?" She turned to take out her clothes, the process slower with one hand holding the towel to her chest.

"The door wasn't locked," Vikram said.

Nikhil began laughing and couldn't stop.

"Don't look away or go out on my account, please make yourself at home." She went inside the bathroom, muttering to herself, "Now I'll have to buy a bathrobe."

When Esha came out, dressed in blue track pants and a white sleeveless tee, Nikhil was nowhere to be seen and Vikram stood looking out of the window that faced the boundary.

"Don't stand in front of the window." The words were out before she could stop herself.

"It's bulletproof."

"Oh... Still, why should we let anyone know which part of the residence you are in?" She pulled the curtains closed.

"You suffer from paranoia."

"Why do you always resist my... my..."

"Commands..." he supplied the word, moving towards her. He traced her lower lip with his thumb and her heartbeat started trotting at an uneven pace. "You know half of the people I meet become tongue-tied in front of me and almost all the people in my family are afraid of me. And here you are. Leave aside fear, you order me around."

"It must be because I don't need anything from you except to... you know... to follow orders." She couldn't help as a smile sneaked on her lips at the last phrase.

"Are you sure?"

"Huh...?"

"That you don't need anything from me."

"Can we be serious on this subject?"

"I'm serious. After all, it's my life. Isn't it?"

"That's what I'm saying."

"I understand what you are saying, sweetheart. But you know I'm not afraid for my life now. I used to be once, when there was all kind of security around me in the boarding school, in the US. Cowering behind other people. Risking the lives of people assigned to my security. But one day I thought what was I, Vikramaditya Seth, doing about my fear? What was I afraid of? They are also human beings... the criminals, aren't they? They are strong so I made myself stronger. They have guns so I got a gun too and made it a point to excel in shooting."

"But they have the element of surprise on their side."

"Yes, for that I have Nikhil and... you." Vikram smiled. "You know the other thing that I have on my side? I have done everything in my life. There's nothing I haven't done. And don't think I'm suicidal. I have that primal instinctive caution to preserve my life, which keeps me safe from tripping down the stairs, but I'm not afraid... but no, that's not entirely true..." He stepped forward and pulled her to him by the waist, in intimate contact from toe to chest. "I'm scared... not for my life but for the people whom I love."

Esha stared at him, mesmerized, her chest rising and falling rapidly.

"How is the shoulder?" He ran his finger lightly on her shoulder taking care not to touch the wound. His breath fanning her face.

Her throat felt like charred coal and she swallowed. "They removed the stitches two days back. It'll be fine in a week's time."

Keeping one hand on her nape, he placed his lips over hers in a hard, demanding contact. She froze. His lips felt hard yet warm coaxing her to open her mouth. The whiff of tobacco hit her, galvanizing her to push at his chest. A desperate push. He released her immediately and she sneezed clutching her shoulder. One, two, three...

"Don't tell me you are you allergic to kissing."

"To... to... tobac-cco...," she said in between the flood of sneezes and sniffles.

He waved his hand in the air. "Now that's great... I can't quit smoking... do I have to?"

"What a ridiculous conversation!" she said when she was through with the sneezing bout. "I think—"

"I was discussing with Nick, you are not to accompany me anywhere outside the office or after office hours."

"What will be the point then?" She scowled.

"I don't want you in danger's way."

"What about Nick?" Anger reared its ugly head. "He is your friend, best friend, isn't he? Or is it something to do with testosterone?"

He smiled, combing his fingers through his hair. "No, but it's a dilemma. He is what he is, but you have become—"

"We are digressing." She didn't want to hear anything about herself. "I don't agree with whatever you are suggesting. You'll have to fire me if you want me out of the role."

"Fire you? Yeah, that's a swell idea. But for now, let's park the thought." He chuckled and lifted his hand to touch her cheek. Esha stepped back and he dropped his hand. His lips curved in a mild smile, eyes hooded as he regarded her for a moment. "Sleep tight, we leave for Alibaug tomorrow evening." He moved towards the door and closed it behind him with a salute.

The tobacco laced kiss and the pressure of his mouth lingered for a long time with Esha. She closed her eyes, sniffled, and cautioned herself for the umpteenth time to not get involved, hoping against hope that her heart would pay heed to it.

October 29th

Vikram insisted on 'getting some damn privacy' and drove his Lamborghini that day to Alibaug. He made Esha sit with him as the other two cars trailed them. He drove with easy confidence without speeding the massive car, enjoying the ride.

"You have not spoken a single word since we started." He threw a glance at her before concentrating back on the road.

She dug her nails into her palm and looked outside her window.

"Esha, do you generally speak less or is it my influence?"

"You have a gigantic ego." She decided to give it back to him. "What are the security arrangements at the farmhouse?"

He grimaced. "That's a great conversation topic too. Well done. Bet you already know them. But manners have been drilled into me from the day I was born so I will comply with the lady's demands."

Elated to rattle him, she mentally punched the air.

"On one side is the beach, of course," he began. "Apart from that, we own most of the land around the house. The two adjacent farmhouses are owned by friends. There is no way anyone can see the house or the surrounding gardens from those properties. We have men guarding the premises, and there are dogs too. And I'll wear the bulletproof jacket even if I die of humidity." He took out a bottle of vodka from somewhere near the driver's seat, drank straight from it, then held it out to her.

Frowning, she took the bottle and placed it in the slot on her side.

"What? At least let me drink!"

"If you want to drink, then I'll drive."

"No way, no one drives my weakness other than me. Grab the box at the back, I think *dada* must have packed a hamper, let's have a coke or something." He undid his tie, tossed it towards her, and opened the top two buttons of his shirt.

Esha caught the tie on reflex. Her heart stuttered at the intimacy of the act and she threw it over her shoulder as if it was a wriggling snake. She opened the Coke cans, placed one in the cup holder for him, and took a sip from hers.

"So... who all do you have at home?"

She sighed. "You know that already, it is all there on my file."

"That's an emotionless report. Who is Samar?"

"He is... was my boyfriend. And we were too poor to leave our respective responsibilities aside and marry. So we ended the relationship," she replied, her voice devoid of any feeling.

"And he is marrying now?"

"Yes."

"And you? Aren't you free of your responsibilities yet?"

Uncomfortable with baring her life to him, she lost her cool. "Why so many questions? What do you want from me?"

"Pity you are asking me this when I'm driving. I could've shown you instead." He continued when she didn't respond. "I told you, you fascinate me. And I have read your file... so to cut the story short in plain nutshell, I'm hitting on you."

"I think we had discussed that earlier."

"But that was before you took a ... no two bullets for me."

"Then keep hitting and let your head get injured." She turned and looked outside.

He laughed throwing his head back. The sound felt good to her ears and Esha found herself smiling too. It was good to hear him laugh. She hadn't seen him laughing ever since she had been here, or even in the photos, she saw on the Internet. Come to think of it, she had never seen him having fun. Granted there were some extremely beautiful women hanging on his arms every time the media covered him, but even attending those social events was work. He probably never had time to have fun. She clamped down a colossal urge to ask him about what he did during a normal holiday.

"To hell with your argument!" he said when he got his breath back.

"It is human psychology. The more emotionally one is involved with the subject, the more irrational decisions one takes at the time of stress."

"I object to the word 'subject' for me." He threw a quick glance at her, a faint smile on his lips.

"I know you are used to getting everything you want, but by now, at your age, you have to understand that people don't get everything they want."

He chuckled. "I understand that... I haven't had a cigarette in the past six hours."

Her heart dropped to her stomach. This was breaking news! Embarrassed, Esha didn't know what to say to that, so she changed the topic.

"Who do Nick and you suspect?"

He sighed. "Right now, we don't have any suspect."

Vikram fell silent after that, lost in his own thoughts.

Esha wasn't sure if she was relieved or disappointed.

⟶•⟨•⟩•⟵

ALIBAUG, MUMBAI
29TH OCTOBER, 7:22 PM

They entered the sprawling property around seven p.m. The wide expanse of the landscaped gardens had a calming effect after being subjected to the concrete jungles of Mumbai city. Esha's eyes feasted on the sprawling opulence of the two-story bungalow with its own swimming pool and tennis court. At the center of the garden was a helipad with the Seths' logo painted on the concrete floor. As she got off the car, she heard a horse neigh. There was a stable as well!

"Welcome to paradise," Vikram said. He was clearly proud of his home. "My best childhood memories are associated with this house." He looked around and took a deep breath. "Here both of us, *di* and I, would get my parents' undivided attention. Will you prefer to rest or to take a look around?"

"Hello, Mr. Seth," Reema, his mother's secretary, joined them before Esha could reply. "Chhotu, take Ms. Esha's luggage to the guest house," Reema instructed to the young man, who it seemed was the main caretaker of the farmhouse.

"Guest house?" Vikram frowned. "I had specifically told mamma that Esha is staying in the main house."

Reema looked uncomfortable. "Ms. Urvi and Mrs. Seth had to change a few things."

"I'll be fine at the guest house." Esha tried to intervene.

"Esha stays in the main house," he said.

"Sir, there is a shortage of rooms."

"Give her mine," he snapped.

Reema's eyebrows went up for a minuscule second before she checked her reaction like the professional she was. Chhotu heard the altercation with avid interest, but his eyes studied only Esha.

"Please... I'm fi—" Esha tried to intervene.

"Sir, we'll manage don't worry." Reema did some mental calculations before she replied in a crisp, professional tone.

"Thanks, Reema. I know I can always count on you. Chhotu, please take the luggage to the main house."

"Yes, sir." A smiling Chhotu bobbed and took care of all their suitcases.

"Come, I have a surprise for you unless you want to rest." Vikram took Esha's arm.

"No, I'm fine."

They began walking on the paved pathway past the back gardens, to the swimming pool.

It was indeed quite a reclusive property, flanked by the highway and the beach on two sides and his friends' properties on the other two. But what about friends and guests the family invited? And the servants? Being rich could be complicated. Having means for all kinds of luxuries, and the staff to maintain them and then worry about human failings.

"What about those trees beyond the boundary wall?"

"Quit worrying." He unfastened the top button of his shirt revealing the bulletproof jacket. "Nick made me wear it since he had to go out. I couldn't wriggle out of this after that day."

She smiled. "Good for him or you?"

He grinned and re-fastened the button.

Her heart slammed against her ribcage again. With his hair ruffling in the breeze and that easy grin, he looked young, carefree. The businessman had been left behind in Mumbai. The realization that she was falling for him didn't surprise her. She had seen it coming. Suppressing a sigh she followed him.

The winding stone path led them to the stables on the other side. In the barn, he took her to one of the stalls. A black stallion brayed restlessly as he sensed Vikram's presence.

"Oh boy! I missed you too," he said as the horse nuzzled against his shoulder.

A warm feeling enveloped her heart on hearing the affectionate tone. He looked like a small boy meeting his pet after a long time, talking, rubbing his back, and offering him sugar cubes.

"Esha, meet my buddy Robin. And Robin this is Esha... my..." He looked at her, and left the sentence incomplete with a faint smile.

"Hi, Robin," she said turning towards the horse, ignoring the awkward moment. At this rate, she'd soon turn into a heart patient.

"Do you ride?" he asked.

"Yes, it was part of the training at the academy."

"Great! I'll bring you here again to ride when your shoulder heals completely."

Esha glanced at him, but the stable staff had diverted his attention. Would there be a next time? She wasn't sure.

After spending half an hour in the stable, Vikram showed her the six Dobermans and their kennel. No one except the handlers were allowed to interact with the dogs. Chhotu happily chattered along giving Vikram an update about the property. He was a dedicated man, clearly in love with his boss, like all the other employees.

Later, to her relief and disappointment, the family and the guests had begun to arrive engaging him for the rest of the evening.

Esha's shoulder, by now, had begun throbbing and demanded rest. As she slipped out of the drawing room and went up to her room, she realized she had missed her afternoon meds as well. The large, round tub in the luxurious bathroom beckoned her to drown her aches and miseries.

She groaned as she slipped into the blissful warm water. Her muscles relaxed as the bathing salts worked their magic. The throbbing receded to a dull ache after a few minutes. She massaged the skin around the lesion. The two wounds were an inch apart. The one, where the bullet had skimmed the skin, had healed and didn't ache at all. But the one where it had embedded in the flesh gave trouble if she moved her arm.

Later clad in a denim shorts and a black tank top, Esha relaxed on the recliner in the balcony. She had requested Reema for dinner to be sent to her room and had left the door open. The green expanse of the landscaped gardens no longer soothed her. Watching the family gathering downstairs had triggered a wave of loneliness. She had two siblings and parents who called only if they needed money. The truth that hurt was that they never hid the fact that they needed only her money.

She came out of her reverie when someone lowered the dinner tray on the side table. Her gazed jerked to his face when she noticed the familiar watch and the scar on the arm. "Oh, you shouldn't have!"

"You are in pain." It was not a question, but a statement. "Are you taking your medicines on time?" Vikram asked, touching her hair.

The unexpected affection made her throat swell with self-pity. She couldn't think of anything to say so she nodded and looked at the tray.

"You okay?" He crouched near the recliner.

She swallowed hard and said, "Please don't worry about me. Go to your guests. Please." The last word came out as a whisper. Esha cleared her throat. "I want to be alone."

"Okay." He dropped a kiss on her temple and left.

⚜

October 30th

Vikram stood in the inner balcony overlooking the massive hall, watching the guests assemble for dinner and dance. Owing to the attacks on him, this year, they had decided to host the party indoors.

Almost everyone was present. Vandana *di* looked up and waved, gesturing him to come down. Jindal, as usual stood far from her, taking too much interest in Viraj's girlfriend.

Viraj had apologized and asked for the funds for the expansion once again. Vikram was considering giving him half of what he had asked, with some ground rules thrown in. *Daija*, as usual, fussed over Aaryan, who tolerated her patiently.

Vikram sighed when his eyes couldn't find the one he wanted to see. He had left Esha alone the whole day today, instructing Reema to take care of her. He had taken regular updates, though. She had slept through the morning and woken up at lunch, which was good. She had also taken a walk in the evening, which was even better.

He had watched her sink deep into misery last night. Despite a strong urge to be with her, he had left. She needed that time to brood, to let her guard down, and to relax, alone. He knew she missed her family, and also that her parents were not affectionate with the offspring who took care of the entire family. And his attention had brought that ugly fact to the fore.

Could parents be so heartless? What had happened for things to come to this level? He wished he had the rights to know more about her, and to ease her pain. He wished he could ignore his guests and search for her. Be with her. But he couldn't. He had a few responsibilities as the host tonight.

His only regret in taking charge of his father's empire was that he wasn't able to lavish enough attention on the people he loved. Loved? Was that what it was? Was he falling for her? Or was it just attraction and gratitude for saving his life?

His thoughts, it seemed, conjured her out of thin air when he suddenly spotted her in the doorway wearing the dress he had gifted her. She looked lovely in the ice-blue and silver ensemble, exactly as he had pictured. All of a sudden, the evening started looking up.

⬥⬥⬥

Esha looked around, assessing the gathering. She had spotted Vikram the moment she had entered the large hall but ignored him. More guests had arrived today. She studied each and every person and mentally cleared them from her list of potentially dangerous people.

"Ms. Sinha, you look lovely, m'dear." Jindal stopped her as she made her way towards the table where the canapés were being served.

"Thank you."

"That was some heroic feat you did. Stepping in front of him in the midst of that hail of bullets."

"Where did you hear that Mr. Jindal?"

"Oh, it's all over the newspapers. You are a heroine in the media's eyes."

She smiled. "The media... hmm... I think we shouldn't give too much importance to the media. They have a tendency to exaggerate and glamorize."

"So, tell me how did you land such a plush job? We've never heard about you, no references. And here you are, working directly for Vikram Seth, moving around with his security team."

"Is it such a plush job, Mr. Jindal?"

"Oh, don't answer all my questions with more questions. I'm surprised to see that no one from your family came to see you at the hospital."

"For a man as busy as you, you notice a lot." Esha smiled and prayed for someone to interrupt and rescue her. Her prayers were answered the next moment.

"I see that you were able to make it," Vikram addressed Jindal, handing her a drink.

She wasn't sure what it was but she took it. Anything to distract the pestering man.

"Surely I can't miss an invitation from my wife's dear brother," Jindal drawled, raising his glass.

"Well then, please enjoy." He gestured at something across the hall. "Mamma wanted to talk to Esha. Please excuse us." He kept his hand at the small of her back.

Jindal looked at them his gaze oscillating between the two, then smiled slowly. "Hmm... so this is the way it is.

Seth Jr. has got a new toy? Ms. Sinha, make sure you milk him for whatever the two bullets are worth."

Vikram's hand on her back fisted. "Sometimes you go too far, Gautam. Please apologize."

Jindal smirked and raised his glass. "My apologies, ma'am," he said and turned to address Urvi's mother, who approached him with a wide smile.

That stung. The remark was aimed to insult. And insult it did, leaving a bad taste in Esha's mouth. She had never been accused of being a gold-digger. Did the Seth family and the world see her in the same light now?

"Esha, please." Vikram steered her towards the pillars. "Don't pay attention to him. He's a nasty man."

"What's this?" she asked raising her glass.

"A virgin mojito. You are taking medicines and shouldn't have alcohol." He smiled and escorted her to a secluded part of the hall. "I knew the dress would suit you."

"Well, I didn't have anything else... er... suitable."

"You don't have to justify. It's yours."

"Will Nick come back tonight?"

He nodded, sipping his drink.

"I want to go back to Mumbai," she blurted.

"Why? Is there a problem here?"

"No. I don't—"

"Vikram, are you still talking work?" Urvi sauntered in looping her hand through his arm. "Come on, you should relax a little. Mamma wants to talk to you. Ms.

Sinha, you can enjoy too. By the way, Reema was looking for you."

With that remark, Esha was deftly reminded of her place in the hierarchy of the Seth Empire. Urvi pulled at Vikram's hand. He resisted but gave up when he saw his mother coming towards them and allowed Urvi to lead him into the thick of the action.

Esha saw the tableau of the rich unfolding and was reminded about the wide gap between her world and theirs. Why did she choose to wear his gift? What was she thinking? It was all a dream. She kept the glass on a little table near the door and left the hall. A breath of fresh air and then sleep was what she needed at this hour.

As she walked in the gardens, the pointed heels kept sinking in the gap between the stones on the paved path, so she took the stilettos off. Dangling them between her fingers, she walked towards the stable instead. The cold earth cooled down the indignation simmering all over her body.

Her phone rang. Vikram was calling, but she ignored it.

The sound of people talking in muted tones fell on her ears, but her curiosity piqued when she heard a feminine voice. The same eerie feeling that she had experienced in Jindal's office crept up on her, making her shiver. Her heartbeat accelerated. She had to know the source, only then would she would be able to breathe normally.

In a hurry to locate the source of her unease, Esha knocked a bucket kept at the entrance of the stable. The voices stopped. Immediately, she heard a set of footsteps running away and another one coming towards her. The feeling intensified. She slipped her hand in her pocket and curled her fingers around the cold, hard metal of the Glock. Robin snorted and shuffled on his feet. She was glad that she had taken her sandals off. She took off the safety clip of the gun still in her pocket.

A small round figure stumbled across her path and fell down at her feet. The eerie feeling faded away at the same rate it had crept on her, one second at a time.

"Aah..."

"Oh *daija*... are you all right?" Esha pulled her hand out of the pocket and lifted the old woman up. "Hope you aren't hurt." One of the stable hands came running as he saw them.

"No... no..." The old woman panted and tried to straighten but couldn't. She sat on the ground again with a moan. "I was just talking to the staff about the horses. Very cute creatures. I like them."

"Yes, of course. But I think you have sprained your ankle." Since the lady couldn't walk, Esha made her sit on a rickety stool that she found nearby. "Take it easy. I'll call someone." Esha called Reema over the cell and relayed the mishap.

Daija sat there and pulled up her sari a bit to examine her rapidly swelling ankle. A bruise was building up on her shoulder too, on the side she had fallen. She also had a tear in her blouse. Though Esha couldn't see clearly, the old lady had a tattoo on her shoulder. Partially visible, it was green in color, the way villagers got it done in India, since time immemorial. When she caught Esha eyes on her shoulder, she became conscious and pulled up her sari *pallu* covering herself.

Reema came along with Chhotu who took *daija* to her room.

Esha's phone rang. Vikram's name flashed on the screen again. She let it ring. If she could she would have switched the phone on mute, but that was against the security protocol. She went on to explore the grounds instead, waiting for her instinct to pick up a scent of whatever had triggered the creepy cold feeling. Nothing happened.

She returned to her room after a long, unsuccessful hunt.

October 31st

"Where were you the whole evening yesterday?" Vikram snapped the moment he saw Esha at the breakfast buffet. She hadn't expected to see him so early in the morning after the late night party.

"Just here and there." She continued to serve herself moved away from him.

"I thought since you've rested the entire day we'll be able to spend a few hours together in the evening but you took off and didn't even take my calls."

"I thought this weekend was an off for me."

"Of course it is, and I'm not talking about work! Dammit, Esha."

Esha stared at her plate, fighting off her anger at Jindal's insinuation, fighting her jealousy with Urvi and Karisma, and fighting her attraction to him. She felt helpless even though she knew that none of these people deserved a place in her mind. She had lost Samar because of her family and now she was exposing herself to another heartbreak.

Vikram took a deep breath. "Listen Esha, I—"

"Was there any girl in the past who would want to take revenge?" The idea had been taking root in Esha's mind since the time she had seen Koel with that man at Marine Drive.

His eyebrows went skywards.

"Someone you had hooked up with who'd be mad enough to try to kill you or hire someone to kill you?" Esha clarified when she got no response from him.

"Hooked up with?" Vikram held her arm and glared. "What do you mean?"

"I meant—"

"You mean to say that I sleep around with anyone and everyone? What impression you have of me? That I don't have any scruples or morals?"

"I don't think about you or your kind... at all." She bit her cheek at her rudeness, but the words had done the damage.

"My kind! My kind..." He snatched the plate from her, handed it to a passing maid and pushed her against the wall. She flinched when pain seared in her shoulder. He released her immediately but placed his hands on the wall caging her from both the sides. "Esha, many a times, and I mean many... I feel like wringing your neck." He closed his eyes and exhaled. "I have not thought about Karisma, since the time you barged into me."

"As if I give a damn—" This was going out of hand.

He glared at her, enough to make her squirm, then straightened to his full height. "Fine. I'm sorry I bothered you with my... my unwanted attention. You'll always have my gratitude for saving my life. Hope you enjoy the rest of your vacation."

With those parting lines thrown at her face, he stormed up the stairs.

Vikram wanted to smash something. No, he wanted to shake some sense into Esha. Why couldn't she accept that he cared for her? Why was she so standoffish? Always. He had thought he was making some kind of headway during the drive yesterday, but no. All his intuition, his experience had failed to tackle their relationship. Relationship? Hah!

Raised voices from his mother's room pulled him away from his frustrations.

Vandana *di* said something, to which his mother had replied with a sharp 'no'. Vikram had never heard his mother being so harsh to his sister. Why was she angry with her? As it is, *di* was going through a bad phase with Jindal fooling around with other women.

"I asked you a question," *di* shouted.

"Ask away, but I'm not obliged to answer any stupid question that you throw at me," his mother replied.

Vikram couldn't remain a mute spectator any longer and entered the room. His mother was ready for the day as usual, but *di* was still in her nightgown.

"What is it? Is Gautam bothering you again?" he asked.

"I don't know what's got into her!" His mother exclaimed as she sat behind her working desk. She picked up a file and began studying it.

"Nothing has got into me, please..." Vandana raised her hand. "Vikram... Have you ever felt that there is something wrong with our family?" she added hurriedly when he raised his eyebrows. "I mean, wrong as in unnatural... not normal... especially mamma and dad's attitude towards me?"

"She is talking nonsense," his mother said without lifting her head from the file in which she was making some notes with a pencil.

"Why are you saying this, *di*? Of all the things... that too about dad..." His worry increased on seeing her so agitated. He prayed that she wasn't coming down with another anxiety attack.

"I have to ask, Vikram. Look at me properly. Do you think I resemble anyone?"

"What kind of question is this? Of course, you do..."

"No, I don't!" She slapped at his hand. "You are lying... mom is dark... I'm fair. She is so tall, magnificent... strong. I'm so weak. I'm unable to handle anything in my life. Even my kid is being brought up by *daija*. Don't you think we are as different as a rabbit and a panda?"

Vikram let out a forced chuckle to normalize the tense atmosphere. "What an example, *di*! Are you fishing for compliments?"

"Don't change the subject. Aren't we? Different, I mean."

"Who has filled your head with such nonsense?" Mrs. Seth slapped the pencil down on the ornate table. "Why are you so low on self-esteem? Have you forgotten that you were crowned the 'Miss India'? You manage all branches of the Jindal Charitable Trust along with being the brand ambassador of one of the finest and most popular perfume brands. Do we need to remind you of your accomplishments every now and then?"

"I have done all these things with your help." Vandana was on the verge of losing her cool again.

Vikram sighed loudly.

"What I have done for you is not called 'help', it is called 'parenting'." Mrs. Seth smiled when Vikram made the truce sign with his hand behind *di's* back. "Come on Vani, you are being too hard on yourself. Enjoy life as it comes, don't think too much."

To their relief, Vandana's phone rang at that moment. The number flashing on the screen brought an instant smile to her face. Silently apologizing to them, she hurried out of the room.

"What brought that on?" Vikram asked his mother.

"If I had my way, I would have fired that nanny of hers. I don't know what Vani sees in her. She is a complete imbecile and fills Vani's ears with all the village mumbo-jumbo."

"Why, *daija* is a harmless little being!"

"Well, I have a different view on that."

⇒·≺⊹◈⊹≻·⇐

KAMATHIPURA DISTRICT, MUMBAI
31ST OCTOBER, 11:00 PM

Nikhil watched the men exchange the packets—a large and a smaller one, money and drugs, he assumed. Reluctantly, he looked away. He had come with a purpose to the dark, tiny pub. Keeping up the pretense of a middleman, he took a swig from the cheap whiskey that was being served and tried not to wince. He didn't know what kind of germs he was subjecting his body to.

Nikhil looked at his watch. It was eleven thirty. The man had promised to meet him at eleven. The contact was to be initiated by them. Nikhil figured they might be scoping him out from a camera. He was in a subtle getup, just in case someone recognized him. Not that he was much in the media, but still it was a precaution he had taken. He looked his watch again and thought he'd wait for another ten minutes.

No one came. The whole day was wasted. Leaving a reasonable sum of money that would cover the cost of his drink and some tip, he left the dark, sultry place.

He sat in the taxi. The driver turned on the ignition.

Boom!

Nikhil didn't feel a thing. His last thoughts were about Vikram and his security. In his single-minded goal of Vikram's safety, he had left a loophole. He didn't get a backup for himself.

He never thought that he would become a target.

⸻⸱≼♦♦≽⸱⸻

PART THREE:CRESCENDO

October 31st

"Vikram... Vikram... don't go out." Esha took a step towards him.

"Don't." Vikram whirled around and raised his hand, his eyes stone cold. "Don't mess with me, Esha. Just... just leave me alone... just go away." Vikram walked with hurried steps to the beach, as if by racing fast, he could leave the pain behind, he could cheat the raging storm that was about to engulf him in its wake.

Esha nodded at the three security guards and spread her hands wide, instructing them to fan out in a semi-circle behind him. She herself stood at ten paces behind him on the beach scanning the perimeter, ready to take action in case of any danger to his life from land, water, or air.

The area was well lit and the dogs, though leashed, prowled with their handlers. Everyone had left by five in the evening. Vikram and Esha had stayed behind because Vikram had a meeting on Monday with a construction company about a new resort in Alibaug.

They had just received the horrible news.

Esha watched him watching the sea and knew nothing would ease the pain, except the passage of time. All of a sudden, he screamed out loud, head thrown up, and his hands fisted by his side. The guards started towards him, but she shook her head and they went back to their positions.

She felt his agony, his pain, his loss and blinked back the tears filling up her eyes. He needed this privacy to mourn the loss of a close friend, much-needed time, that he might not get once he was back in the rut and under the glare of the media. After a while, he went and sat on a broken bench under the shelter of two palm trees. Esha went and sat beside him.

Vikram was looking down, the salty sea breeze ruffling his hair. Esha followed his line of vision and saw a tiny little crab digging its way inside the sand and then coming out and doing it all over again. She kept her hand over his on the bench. He turned his palm and clasped hers tightly.

"He was like a brother to me," he whispered. A tear fell down on his thigh and got soaked on his trousers. "He was that one corner of my life that was untouched by any expectations, ambitions, demands, or greed. He was that one corner where I could be in peace, be myself without any conditions or pre-conceived notions. Free of all stress and worry." Another tear fell from the other eye.

It was scary to see a person as strong as he cry. She pressed his hand and swallowed her own grief and pain caused by his anguish. In that moment, Esha knew that she was totally, irrevocably in love with him. Her heart jolted with the realization. Goddamn! Oh, what a heady feeling! She felt like taking him in her arms and soothing the pain away. Goddamn!

"Why?" He looked at the sky and swallowed the rest of his tears. "It should have been me."

"Don't... don't let guilt drag you down. Death doesn't need a reason. It comes when it has to come."

"Hah...! Just empty words to ease the weak. I'm going to find those bastards and kill them with my own hands." His hand fisted in her palm. "No. I'm going to feed them slowly to the sharks, limb by limb, as they did to him. They tore him apart... so that... so that I couldn't even see him for one last time and give him a proper send off." He sniffled.

"Vikram please..." Her eyes watered again and this time she was unable to stem the flow. Tears rolled down her cheeks. Esha didn't want him to see her cry and wiped them on her shoulders with a subtle tilt of her neck. Vikram, however, sensed her move and turned to look at her.

"Oh! Don't cry Esha, please. I'm sorry I made you cry, sweetheart." He took her in his arms and patted her shoulder.

She hugged him hard and his dam of grief broke down too. He burrowed his face in her neck, drenching her in the flood of tears and unhappiness. They sat holding each other, each one taking solace from other, bound by a beautiful soul, a dedicated friend, and a wonderful human being.

Totally spent, he released his desperate hold on her and moved away.

"I'm sorry," he said after a moment, as he fidgeted a little, taking a deep breath.

"You aren't expected to be stoic all the time."

"Yeah..." He smirked. "I don't remember the last time I cried like this. Couldn't cry when dad went, keeping a strong façade in front of mom, *di*... the media... not a single tear came. It was, as he would have expected from me."

"My grandmother says tears heal the soul faster."

"Do they? When did she say that?"

"When my elder brother died."

He frowned. "Oh yes, you had an elder brother. What happened?"

"We were going in an auto, my father, brother and me, for my school admission. It was I who insisted that he should come along, I worshipped him like anything. Our auto was hit by a bus. My brother died on the spot, my father lost one of his legs, but I didn't get a single scratch on me." Her voice thickened as she relived the memories and bared her soul to him, something she had never done in front of anyone since the accident twenty-three years ago. "I tried to become the son my father lost but he never forgave me for surviving. My grandmother somehow sensed my guilt and pulled me out of the grief."

He put a hand on her shoulder and squeezed.

"It's okay. It was a long time ago," she said.

"I got to know right now." He pulled her to him and stroked her shoulder looking at the horizon. A few tears sneaked out again.

After making sure the house was locked and secured, she peeped into his room. He was reclining on the La-Z-

Boy with his arm on his eyes, nursing a quarter glass of whiskey. Looking at the color of the liquid, she gathered he was drinking neat. She did a round of the dressing room and the bathroom again, before she checked his gun, the battery of his watch, and the mobile phone.

"I'll be in the next room."

"Esha..."

She stopped near the door.

"Stay with me..."

Her heart stopped, then expanded in her chest. If she refused, he would not ask again. And her heart didn't want to deny anything to him. Not today. Not when he was in this condition.

It was complicated. She was getting entangled more and more in this whirlpool of emotions. She turned and moved towards him knowing it was suicidal. But she had no option. He needed her.

He lifted his arm from his face and held out his hand. His eyes were blood-shot and the naked pain in them brought her heart to her throat. She placed her palm on his.

He pulled her hand and she sat beside him on the recliner, her hip touching his.

"We'll get the DNA tests done. Of the... of the..."

"Yes, of course."

"You know he fancied you."

"Vikram..."

"But stepped back when he saw that I had begun to like you."

"You should try to get some sleep—"

"Nothing helps..." He caressed her lower lip and pulled her towards him. She couldn't resist and leaned, acutely conscious of the pressure of his length against hers. "Make me forget everything Esha..." he whispered, his breath caressing her lips. "Make it go away…" he said, looking forlorn and helpless, waiting for her to make a move.

She closed the distance between their lips. He tasted of whiskey and desperation. Sighing, she put her arms around his neck and deepened the kiss. He shuddered, trailing feather-light kisses all over, their breath mingling.

"You know you are an incredible woman..."

"Remember that in the morning." She smiled to lighten the mood.

He smiled and caressed her face, her lips, then crushed her against his chest. His hands were all over her body, tugging at her clothes, as she yanked at his shirt. She wanted to feel his skin against hers and quivered as the mat on his chest brushed against her breasts. His mouth followed his hands, caressing, kissing, biting, and branding her. Half-heartedly, she tried to slow him down but gave up the fight between sanity and passion.

Somehow, she didn't remember when and how, in the middle of the frenzy, they moved to the bed. She remembered asking him about protection. He grunted and took care of it. It was as if they were both starved for each other, wanting to be one with a fervor she had never felt, ever. Together, they reached the heights of passion, sweating and panting despite the air-conditioning. She smiled at the direction of her thoughts as she gathered her breath.

He kissed her, slowly, leisurely in the aftermath. Tears gathered in her eyes at the tender way in which he cradled her in his arms after the passionate, almost violent, lovemaking. He stroked and caressed her back, and waist, and didn't let her go even as he drifted to a restless sleep.

She lay there, listening to his uniform breathing and felt his limbs loosen. It was humbling that she had been able to bring him the comfort he craved. But what after this, Esha wondered.

A part of her soul would get ripped from her and remain with him when the danger would be over and she would have to leave. He would go back to his world of Urvis and Karismas and she would have to live with the remaining half and survive without him, aching and hurting. A tear escaped her eye. She took a deep breath and swallowed the rest.

Major Esha Sinha never cried.

━━━━◆◆◆◆◆━━━━

Her eyes snapped open and the gun was in her hand. It was pitch dark inside the room. All was still and silent, but something had woken her up, something that she couldn't ignore. The wrist-watch showed the time. It was a little shy of five a.m. The echo of a dog's bark shattered the silence, once. Eyes and ears tuned to any unnatural sound, she searched for her top, but found his shirt instead. For a second, her senses recalled their passionate jaunt almost four hours back, but she made herself concentrate on any unnatural sound outside as she put on the shirt.

Gun in hand, she parted the curtains fractionally and scanned the balcony and the gardens beyond. The sun was beginning to make its presence felt as the twilight gave way to the first rays of the sun. But there was no movement or sound. She could see one of the dogs roaming leisurely, sniffing here and there. Apart from the ferocious canines, there was no one up and about. What had disturbed her? She had complete confidence on her sixth sense. Someone was watching them. Someone was out there.

Vikram had woken up the moment she had left the bed. The first thought that hit him brought an excruciating wave of pain to his chest. Nikhil was gone. He closed his eyes. The grief was unbearable.

The click of the gun brought him back from the cloud of sorrow to her comforting presence.

He opened his eyes and followed her movements across the room, eyeing her silhouette—sexy in his shirt that was a little large for her. She held the gun, confident and alert, as she continued her watch behind the translucent lace curtains of the full-length glass window. The garment slipped to one side baring one smooth shoulder and part of her arm. He had never experienced anything more erotic than the sight of her lean frame in his white shirt, holding a gun. He felt the stirring of desire through his veins, again.

"Why are you up?" he asked making her jump a little.

"Something woke me up. I think I should go and check with Jay," she answered without taking her eyes off from the view outside.

"Don't be silly, whosoever is after my life won't murder me in my own bed. Don't you realize they want to make it look like an accident or an outside job? Come back, we have at least two hours before dawn. I want to sleep with you."

That got her attention and she glanced at him, a smile tugging at the corners of her mouth. "Not very subtle about your wants, are you?"

"Just a victim of your charm. Never thought my shirt will make you look so desirable."

Esha's heart galloped as her throat went completely dry at the way he looked at her. Knowing her voice wouldn't support her if she tried to say anything, she walked towards the bed. Keeping the gun down, she leaned over him.

"I never knew I would develop such a fetish for bodyguards." He traced her brows and brought a finger to a corner of her mouth.

"What are we doing, Vikram?" she croaked somehow.

"Making love."

"As it is, things are too complicated," she whispered.

"Then let's complicate them some more. I love tangles and twists." He kissed the corner of her mouth, where his finger was. His hand went inside the shirt and spanned her waist.

She couldn't help but take the support of the bed.

"I love your hair, your skin. I love the way you lisp, and these eyelashes."

She smiled. "You like my eyelashes? This is the weirdest compliment I have ever received."

"How many people have complimented you?" he asked pulling and pinning her under him on the bed. He touched his lips to hers and said, "No don't tell me, I hate them already." He touched his lips to her nape.

He was finding her glamorous because she was the exact opposite of what he had encountered throughout his life. Esha sighed and gave in to her feelings, brushing aside all thoughts of caution and the subsequent dangers of getting deeply involved with him. She would worry tomorrow.

"Stop thinking and touch me," he whispered, bringing her hand to his chest.

He had picked up the right spot on her neck and she tilted her head to give him easy access to everything. His hands were caressing the sides of her breasts. She yearned for him to take them in his hand, but somehow he knew how to tantalize her the most, prolonging the pleasure. His lips and tongue on her nape and ears were driving her beyond the precipice of sanity.

She slid both her hands on his shoulders. He was all hard muscle, taut and strong. She ran her hands over his biceps, then back on his shoulders, before she fisted them in his hair and brought his mouth up close. She looked in his eyes and nipped his lips. He slid his hands under her hips and pulled her closer, showing her his need as he darted his tongue inside her mouth. Esha moaned and gave in to the assault.

Vikram didn't know what had hit him. On one hand, he wanted to leisurely explore her body and on the other, he was losing control of the whole game. Her hands on his body singed him. He looked at her closed eyes and at her upturned, small yet sexy breasts inviting lust as he had never experienced before. He felt like a teenager all over again as he took one of her breasts in his mouth and suckled. She moaned again, her hands on his head now. He stroked her flat stomach, lean thighs and touched her inner core. As her hips arched towards his hand, he placed his mouth on hers.

She came alive in his arms.

"Vikram... please," she groaned against his lips.

"Take it easy... slowly darling... we have all the time in the world."

Four hours earlier he had selfishly taken what she had offered, but now he wanted to give her a night to remember. He wanted to brand her with his touch. She was his to love, forever. Yes, forever. She moaned and her breath hitched as the orgasm hit her, wave after wave. He left her for protection and then, placing his body over hers, slowly entered her. Her hips welcomed the intrusion and she sighed against his lips, allowing him to take her over the peak of pleasure again.

⸺◈⸺

November 1st

Esha stirred in the bed, and her elbow poked into Vikram's stomach. He grunted and threw an arm around her waist pulling her closer. She caressed his arm and felt a faint ridge high up on his upper arm. She took a peek at the skin and found a square inch of a patch that she would have missed if it hadn't been of a different shade. Slightly darker than the rest of the skin.

Wondering about the change in color, she looked up and found him awake, watching her. He understood her curiosity.

"As I had told you earlier, I was kidnapped... when I was nine." He turned her around and kissed her, then continued. "I was taken somewhere near the Nepal border and held in captivity—for ransom, I guess, though my parents never got any call or a note. Cutting the story short, I managed to escape somehow and was found by some kind men who took me to the police." He held out the other arm. "These scars are from the fence of the small cottage I was held in. The only thing I remember from that ordeal was the layout of the cottage and a pattern tattooed on my arm, which was the same as the one on my kidnapper's arm. As far as I remember it was a symmetrical geometric design, but ugly."

The incident he narrated reminded her about the tattoo she had seen on *daija's* shoulder, but that was curved as far as she could recall. She traced the skin, waiting for him to continue.

"I often had nightmares. Psychologists advised for plastic surgery on the pattern to forget the trauma. After the surgery, I was sent abroad for further studies and out of harm's way."

"You don't remember his face?"

"No, he had a mask on all the time. He wore a short-sleeved t-shirt though, because of which I could see that he had the same pattern tattooed on the inside of his lower arm."

"And these?" She caressed the scars on his cheek.

"These are from the mountain accident."

"I want to see the tattoo design."

Vikram smiled and kissed her again. "What will you do with that? It is all in the past now."

"Just curious." Esha pushed at his chest. "Please."

"Okay. The sketch is in the police records and in our files too. I'll arrange for a copy for you," he said and tried to engage her in a fight of tongues again.

She pushed him away and looked at her wristwatch. "Shouldn't we be getting up? It's twelve past ten." To her regret, her remark instantly brought the shadow of yesterday's tragedy back onto his face, as he sighed and loosened his hold on her.

⊂•≼⧫⧫≽•⊃

After a cold shower in the adjacent ensuite bathroom, Esha was ready to move. Her head was pounding with the lack of sleep and confused emotions. It all made her clumsy—a state of mind she wasn't happy about. She had unclipped and re-clipped the magazine from the gun two times. Then she remembered that she had forgotten her wrist watch in Vikram's room. She didn't want to face him after last night, but had no choice.

She cautiously opened his room. The shower running in the bathroom indicated he was up and getting ready.

Esha picked up her watch lying on the side table and heard the click of the door opening. Vikram stood there with dripping hair and a towel around his waist. His red eyes went over her hurriedly before he turned towards the cupboard.

He pulled out his clothes, a pair of blue jeans, and a white t-shirt. "Let's go. Mother's called me around twenty times. She won't rest until she sees me and I have to make arrangements."

The shadow of Nikhil's death haunted his eyes once again.

"Esha, I want you to go back."

Angry and hurt, she glared at him.

"I'm not saying this lightly. I relieve you of all your duties as of now. We'll settle the full and final payment electronically. You'll be compensated for the full three months with a bonus." He didn't look at her through the entire monologue and continued dressing. He clipped on his watch. "You are to go back to Delhi as soon as possible."

"No," she said. He looked tired and dejected. It wrenched her heart to see him in that condition.

His head jerked at her voice and he finally looked at her. It was heartening to see the habitual glint of steel, when someone didn't agree with him, appear in his eyes. "Well, didn't you listen? You are fired."

"And you are an idiot if you think I'm going to leave your side for even a second."

"The decision is not open for discussion, Major." He sat on the bed and pulled on his socks.

"I no longer work for you. Remember I have been fired. I can do anything I want."

He threw the sock down, covered the two steps between them, and pulled her to him, hugging her hard. She let him hold her and returned the hug. Then as suddenly he had caught her, he loosened the hold and rested his forehead on hers. "I can't afford to lose you, Esha. I'll be destroyed if anything happens to you."

She touched his cheek. "Nothing will happen, trust me." She squeezed his arms. "Please."

Unmoving, he stood holding her in his arms for a few seconds before his phone interrupted the moment. "Yes, mom. I'm coming. Just starting from here."

He put on his shades donning back his stoic, public avatar along with it. "Is the chopper here?"

"Yes."

"Let's go."

⸻⸱≺◄◆►≻⸱⸻

OUTHOUSE, SETHS' RESIDENCE, MUMBAI
1ST NOVEMBER, 11:45 PM

Esha studied the drawing Vikram had arranged to be delivered to her room that night. As he had said it was symmetrical. Though it didn't make any sense to her, she was drawn to it every time she lay her eyes on it. Something niggled at the back of her mind but she couldn't quite place it. Lost in her thoughts, she glanced outside the window.

Everything was quiet. It seemed, even nature mourned for Nikhil. It had hit her too when she had gone past his room on the ground floor earlier in the evening. The house felt strange and empty. According to the police and Uday's report, the bomb was crude and made by a novice, but it had done its job. She had cried again in the privacy of her room. There would be no one who would call her Xena.

They had visited Nikhil's parents that afternoon.

"His life was yours," Nikhil's father had uttered that single sentence and had proceeded to console Vikram, who had broken down again holding Nikhil's mother in his arms. It wrenched her heart to see them consoling Vikram, instead.

Vikram had stayed back with his mother that night, and Esha had returned to the apartment after reviewing the security arrangements. She didn't give a damn about her cover anymore. Jay didn't question when she took over Nikhil's role. Apparently, he had guessed her position. *'Nikhil had planned for all contingencies except his own safety,'* Esha thought, her heart heavy with grief.

Her gaze went back to the drawing again. Why did it pull at her guts? She was sure she had never come across a pattern like this in her lifetime, but why did her brain refuse to let go of the niggling instinct? Even after a lot of thinking and repeated attempts to forget about it, the feeling refused to subside and it frustrated her. Esha decided to make coffee.

Slapping the drawing on the side table, she moved towards the kitchenette. The paper fluttered under the fan. She lunged forward and caught it. Anchoring it with the novel, she lit the stove to make the much-needed cup of coffee.

As she turned with her coffee mug, her gaze landed on the table. She froze. *Daija's* nude shoulder flashed again in her mind, stunning her with the magnitude of its implication.

Esha shifted the book slightly to reveal a-third of the design and looked at it one more time. Then she curved the paper slightly as if it was etched on a round surface. Though slightly bigger the portion clearly matched to the one she had seen on *daija's* shoulder in Alibaug. The only difference was the ink color and size.

Daija! The nanny. The old woman. A killer? A skilled sharpshooter? Dealing in explosives?

The pieces did not belong to the same puzzle, Esha frowned.

Or maybe she was looking at it from the wrong angle. Taking a sip from her coffee, she blanked her mind and reconsidered the facts.

The tattoo on Vikram's arm was done when he was kidnapped. He was nine at that time. There was no ransom call, which meant the kidnappers were not after money. Did they want to include him in their cult? Did *daija* follow some cult?

Scampering on the other side of the bed, she pulled out *daija's* file from the drawer. It didn't mention anything about any weird religious inclination. *Daija* had been employed a few days before Aaryan was born. Was there a connection with Vandana? She definitely stood to gain a lot if Vikram died.

She knew Vikram's history by heart. He was sent abroad to the US at ten years of age. He remained there for fourteen years. There was no dangerous event or accident reported around him in the US. He was involved in a minor car accident due to his own negligence and had done community service there. That meant the killers didn't have the means to go abroad.

The second attack happened after eight years of his living in India! This one aimed not to kidnap him but to end his life. A hale and hearty child appealed to them more than the adult heir to a large empire. Why such a huge time gap between the attacks? Was it possible that there were two different forces in the game?

Esha opened everybody's dossiers and scattered them all over the bed.

Aaryan was born the year Vikram had come back to India and *daija* had come into their lives in the same year. What a perfect coincidence! But why did it take them eight years to launch an attack?

Wait a minute! Vikram and Nikhil had met during a trek and Vikram had saved Nikhil's life. Was that really an accident? Was the rope that gave way meant for Nikhil or was it meant for Vikram?

Esha jumped up from the bed and wrote all her hunches as she would write a crime board. It was possible that *daija* could be an accomplice or the mastermind. Esha recalled that she was speaking to someone that night in the stable. Who could that be? Did that mean that the killer had access to Vikram throughout that weekend? She shuddered at the thought. And she had left him all alone most of the time during those two days—engrossed in her own misery and jealousy. See that's what emotions do to a person, she chided herself. One forgets to be objective and drops their guard.

The tattoo pattern didn't make complete sense, but at least they had something to go on with. She picked up the phone and dialed Vikram's number

"Hey!"

His groggy voice reminded her that it was one a.m. in the night. Shucks. "Oh, I'm sorry. I forgot it was so late. You go off to sleep, please." This could have been discussed a few hours later, Esha thought as she virtually smacked her head.

"You have woken me up, so now you have to pay a fine," he drawled.

"Fine? What kind of a fine?"

"Em... let me think... what about phone sex?"

"Really?" She could picture him smiling, and she too relaxed back on the bed.

"Yeah..."

"I have no idea about phone sex."

"Hmm... let me train you."

"Okay."

"You can tell me about what you are wearing... suggestively... in a seductive tone, of course."

"Okay. But what if I'm not wearing anything?"

He groaned and she grinned.

"And I've just had a bath," she continued, "...the water droplets are slowly running down my..." She stopped in a dramatic pause.

"Ah, why did you stop, woman? I was getting there."

Esha found herself aroused at the mere thought. "Come home tomorrow. We'll shower together," she croaked.

He went silent and she bit her lip. The sexual tension between them changed to profound sorrow.

"Vikram?"

"Yeah..." he answered after a couple of seconds.

"Time is the only healer."

"Yeah, right."

"Sleep well."

Murmuring incoherently, he disconnected the call.

Esha didn't tell him about what she had found—her findings could wait for a few more hours.

November 2nd

The pattern matched with the one on *daija's* shoulder! It was unbelievable.

Vikram couldn't digest the news. Esha must have been mistaken. *Daija* had been living with them for the past eight years. She adored Vandana and Aaryan. She received a handsome salary and had no liability. How could she be involved in such a heinous plot? Esha was plain mistaken.

The object of his thought was pinning a note on the pin-board in Vikram's den at home when he entered the room.

Vikram had shifted his office upstairs. It was his idea. There was no safer a place than his house and he wanted her to stay out of harm's way as far as possible. He wasn't letting her out of his sight till this mess was over. Deciding to spearhead the investigations himself, he had cleared his calendar as much as possible. He regretted not having done this before—maybe then Nikhil would have been alive.

Damn! Damn! Damn! This was one war he had to win. He had to avenge Nikhil's death.

"Hey!" he called out when Esha remained absorbed in her notes.

"Hey." She waved a hand without turning. "I can't tell you how intriguing all this is. I feel as if I know the answers to all the questions but they are eluding me like butterflies—so near yet so far out of reach."

"This is the first time you have spoken so many words together without scowling."

"What?" she turned towards him and scowled.

He smiled. It was comforting to have her no-nonsense presence by his side. Maybe he'd ask her to move in with him. He wasn't sure if she'd agree, but he knew he was going to try. But before he could broach the subject, Kishore *dada* ushered Uday in.

The grim lines on Uday's face told Vikram that the loss had affected him too. Uday was one of Nikhil's best friends.

"When are the DNA reports expected?" Vikram asked.

"In 3 to 4 days."

"Can't they be expedited?"

"I'm pulling all the strings," Uday said, then updated them on the investigations. The Delhi shooting trail had gone cold and nothing could be traced beyond what the young girl, Debbie's friend, had told them. The only thing that she would tell them was that he always wore red and white cotton stole around his neck, which was fairly common in India.

After the shooting in which Esha was hurt, his sleuths had been combing the underworld gun parts dealers and Uday had had a meeting with one of the informants last night.

"A man had purchased a few parts from one of the arms dealers but again he had kept his face partially hidden with the muffler which, on that day, was black and white checkered. We have the approximate height and build of the man. He is fair, between forty to fifty years of age, maybe more. Speaks with a rough *pahari* accent, like the people from the hills."

Uday opened another file. "Based on that, we have zeroed in on seven people who have been expelled from the army in the past ten-fifteen years because of various reasons. There are two who have taken premature retirement using flimsy excuses. According to the army records, one thing common between them is that they all were expert marksmen."

Placing the files on the table, Uday studied the crime board Esha had created. "I see you have already done the homework. If we assume that the culprits behind Vikram's kidnapping twenty odd years back and the attacks now are the same, then the tattoo pattern is a vital link. The connection needs to be established with the nanny and the man with the stole, both from the northern region," he said after a while.

"If the incidents are connected, then the motive goes back more than twenty years. We'll have to see who all can have enmity with Vikram's parents," Esha said.

Vikram chuckled, shaking his head. "I think you are mistaken about *daija's* tattoo. The ceiling lights are not good at the stables. And you have seen only part of the pattern."

Esha pursed her lips and chose to remain silent.

"Meanwhile we have received the report on the tattoo design," Uday continued pulling their attention on the last of his reports. "It represents the '*MahaKaali Yantra*' and it stands for seeking blessing from Goddess *Kaali* for conquering one's enemies. According to most sources, it represents a positive blessing to shield one from the negativity in life, but you never know what a convoluted mind may perceive it as."

"And what if the incidents are not connected?" Vikram asked.

"Then we have only one track to follow, the army men and a stole loving person. Still, the nanny's connection cannot be ignored until we have a harmless explanation," Uday said. "A background check would have been done by Jindal's security team when she was hired, but my team is now on her too."

"Let's look at the men for now." Vikram didn't want to discuss anything related to di's family. What if nothing came out? The relationship would get tainted if there was an innocent enough reason for the damned tattoo. But what if something was really amiss? He shook his head. He'd assess the situation with a calm frame of mind before taking a decision.

"Out of the seven, I'm leaning towards these four." Uday selected four files and pushed them forward on the table. "They are all single, have no roots, and have not stayed at one place for long. Though none of the profiles mention a tattoo on their body. Out of the rest, the fifth one was in Rohtak jail at the time of the shooting in Delhi. The sixth one is lame, lost one leg recently in an accident. And the last one is working in an ashram down south and hasn't stepped out of the premises since he had been expelled from the army. You should look at all of them and see if it jogs your memory."

Vikram picked up the first file, while Esha took the second one.

The image of a man stared at Vikram as he turned the cover of the file. The man looked pathetically lean, incapable of wielding a walking stick leave alone a sniper rifle.

"I'll take your leave," Uday said. "I'll come again in the evening and debrief you on the day's progress. Meanwhile Vikram, have your mother take a look at the files too. Esha is right, it could be some old enmity. Shall I put a trail on the nanny?" Uday asked at the door.

"No!" Vikram said then looked at Esha. "No one speaks about this to anyone. This remains between the three of us till I say otherwise. We are still not sure if the pattern is the same."

Uday nodded and left.

Esha didn't even glance up from the file she was reading, though he could see a pulse ticking on her jaw.

Vikram slapped the file in his hand close and added it to the stack on the table. "Leave the files in the safe when you are done, I'll look at them tonight," he said and left the room.

SETHS' RESIDENCE, MUMBAI
2ND NOVEMBER, 10:30 PM

It had been more than 24 hours since she had found about the pattern but still didn't get the go-ahead from Vikram to pursue the tattoo lead. Esha fumed and fretted to act on it, but he refused to break his silence over the issue. She wanted a trail put on the old woman. She had discussed this with Uday and he had sent her the bank statements, phone call logs, and other reports, but none of it raised a red alert anywhere.

The financial statements didn't tell her anything. There was nothing beyond the regular salary and routine withdrawals. She had looked everywhere. Uday had done a meticulous job in furnishing the evidence. She picked up the phone call log again and stared at the time pattern. Rubbing her eyes she stared at the tiny figures. It was a tedious, time-consuming, and headache-inducing job. The numbers swam in front of her eyes. She looked at the clock. It was eleven p.m. She needed to get some sleep. As she prepared for bed, the idea struck her as lightning thunders in the darkest of the skies.

The threat was to Vikram, so why was she sitting closeted in the room? Did she really need his permission? She could always go and do her own sleuthing. She had the security information on Jindal's penthouse. Moreover, the couple of rooms allocated to *daija* were on a separate floor and had a separate entrance.

It was time to do something to bring them a step closer to some concrete evidence.

———◆———

November 3rd

The door clicked open with minimum noise. Familiar with the layout of the staff apartments on the top floor, Esha stood leaning against the door, listening for any sound that might indicate that someone was awake. After five minutes of waiting, she clicked on the camera jammer and entered the two-room dwelling of the nanny.

The night bulb threw a pale blue light on the interiors of the living room, which was stark and minimalistic with a small marble temple in one corner. Her heart hammered in her rib cage as she noticed the black twelve inch Goddess *Kaali* idol placed on the pedestal inside the white carved structure.

Keeping her emotions in check, she moved towards the bedroom. Lying on her side, the old woman was sound asleep. Esha pulled on the mask over her face, took out the chloroform drenched handkerchief and put it over the woman's nose.

After waiting for five-seconds, she took off the handkerchief and un-fastened the old woman's blouse.

OUTHOUSE, SETHS' RESIDENCE, MUMBAI
3RD NOVEMBER, 3:45 AM

Esha froze as she entered her room after an exhilarating few hours. Vikram sat in the easy chair looking at her like a king cobra.

"Hey," she said taking off the latex gloves.

He didn't say anything.

"Aren't you going to ask where I have been?" She took off her black leather jacket.

"Why?" he whispered.

"You'll be amazed at what I found."

"Why shouldn't I wring your neck instead?" he snapped.

"Look, I can't just sit and twiddle my toes waiting for something to happen. I took all the precautions. I had a backup. Uday knew about my trip and his team had been sitting in the van outside monitoring me." She tapped the buckle on her belt that had the camera.

"Do you have any idea how many seconds it takes to snuff out a life? Two bloody seconds!" He stood up so suddenly that she stepped back. "And your shoulder hasn't even healed properly."

"There was no risk." Esha had never seen him so angry. His hands fisted by his sides and his nostrils flared.

"Do you even realize what I went through the moment I came to know you were not here?"

Understanding his anger but unable to face him, she turned towards the tiny fridge. "I had informed Jay too. Didn't he tell you?" Unable to face his accusing gaze, she took out a bottle of water and drank straight from it. He wasn't supposed to know about her excursion. "How come you are here at such an ungodly hour?"

He didn't say anything and only glared at her.

"I'd like to sleep."

He continued to stare at her for a few more seconds, then stormed out of the apartment. She was glad to have escaped his wrath but disappointed that they had parted on a sour note. She wanted to pick his brain on the information she had unearthed. They were so close. Just a few more links to verify and they could nab the killer. She sighed.

Now that the adrenaline was receding, the risk she had taken made her tremble. Hormones were difficult to fathom. She realized that she wanted a warm reassuring hug from him too.

SUBURBS, MUMBAI
3RD NOVEMBER, 5:30 AM

Usually, he played the various surveillance tapes in fast forward while eating his breakfast after the night shift. But today his meal lay forgotten on the floor of the basement room. Ripples of fear tied his stomach in knots when he saw a blip on one of the camera feeds of the staff area at Jindal's residence. The tape had gone blank for almost twenty minutes as if someone had jammed the camera. Or maybe the electricity backup went off too, but that had never happened at Jindal's in the past seven years. He checked the feed of the entrance lobby and lift area. Same problem. Maybe there was a technical glitch.

He quickly checked the other feeds from the main house. His worst fears were confirmed. There was no problem in them.

What had happened? Why had the cameras only at the entrance and in her rooms malfunctioned? Because someone wanted to hide their identity. For what? To search her rooms. Why her? She had never been part of anything, except passing on the money to him, that too not directly.

He picked up the phone and dialed the number—a first when he was calling without the customary missed call. The next moment he disconnected. What if the calls were being monitored?

Where had he gone wrong?

At first, he had planned to rear him like his own child. When that failed and he didn't have another option, he had thought of a clean, painless death. For he, Seth Jr., wasn't to be blamed for being born. The punishment was for the parents. But as time passed, all his plans had crumbled like fragile sand castles. Where had he gone wrong? The answer lay with his Goddess. He stood up and began the preparation for the pooja.

He sat performing the rituals, asking Maa the reason behind so many failures. After an hour of frenzied chanting, he finally had his answer.

Kaali maa wished for supreme sacrifice. She was demanding bali. She wanted the ultimate homage—the blood aahuti—his or his enemy's. If he succeeded, it was Her will, or he'd sacrifice himself.

He picked up the newspaper that carried the news of the weekend party at the Seths' farmhouse at Alibaug.

'The new arm candy of the Seth scion.'

The headline screamed, with a photo of Vikramaditya Jr. and his PA, his bodyguard, he corrected his observation.

The photographer had managed to capture a rare emotion on Seth's face. The way both of them stood looking at each other, there seemed much more between them than just an employee-employer relationship. The thought brought on a wave of disgust. Women were the same everywhere. Spreading their legs, salivating because of a few notes thrown their way. It was time to teach them a lesson. Again.

An idea began taking shape in his mind. Slowly, Maa showed him another path to his revenge.

SETHS' RESIDENCE, MUMBAI
3RD NOVEMBER, 8:00 AM

Esha pinned the scanned copy of the group photograph she had found locked away in the nanny's room and the pattern of the tattoo that she had clicked. Although she had taken the photos in dim light, the results were good. Now there was no doubt that old *daija* was involved. The tattoo on her shoulder matched the one etched on Vikram's arm. The photograph in her safe was of her younger days. She and a boy in his early teens stood flanking a girl elder to both of them.

"What do you think?" she asked the moment Uday entered the room. "I think I have a name. The picture of the boy seems to match with one of your men in the files." She picked up the file and handed it to him. "Shivam Negi."

Uday didn't pay attention to the file and smiled. "I have one more link. The same profile matches with one of the night shift guards assigned to Jindal's office security. Since he was a parttimer, he had escaped our scrutiny earlier." He pinned another blown up recent photograph of both, Negi and the nanny. "Maybe Jindal is funding him or..." He left the sentence incomplete.

They both knew, if Vandana was involved, Vikram would be devastated.

"Great, so that means he is our man and these two might be related. So who is the other girl with them? She is older than them." Her hands on her waist, Esha studied the photographs.

"The army files say that Negi is an orphan. And the nanny's file indicates that she is an only child and a childless widow. No official records of her marriage exist, so we don't have information on her husband. The address given here is of a village near Ranikhet. There is no mention of any other female relative. So who is the other girl?"

"Maybe she is a friend or a teacher." The girl looked smart and well-groomed.

"Also, there are no phone records that connect Negi and *daija*," Uday said.

"But the tattoo does tell us a story. I'm willing to bet my two eyes that the man will also have the same tattoo right where he had marked Vikram."

"I don't want you blind under any circumstance, Major." Vikram stood at the doorway looking at the new evidence on the board. He seemed to have made peace with Esha's excursion last night. "What do we have here? You both seem quite elated."

Uday updated him on the progress they had made last night without taking names of any of the family members. The nanny, Shubha Thapar, and the man, Shivam Negi, were related somehow. Circumstantial evidence pointed to the fact that these two were involved right from his kidnapping. The motive, though, was still to be established.

"My team is also combing the train and plane records to see if he had travelled to Delhi, but I'm sure I'll not find any evidence under his official name. I've sent two of my men to the village in Ranikhet and by evening, we'll get some information on the Negi family. I think you should ask Mrs. Seth to come here." Uday added the last bit in a softer tone. "Maybe she can throw some light on the photograph or the names."

Vikram nodded and stepped to the board, taking a closer look at the photographs.

"We should put a trail on the nanny, Vikram," Uday said.

"Fine." Vikram kept looking at the board.

"Great. I'll come again in the evening for the next update." Uday nodded at Esha and left.

"So, are you happy?" Vikram asked still studying the photos.

"Happy? No. More like relieved. We now have a concrete lead."

"Do you know what this could do to my family?"

She couldn't understand his line of thinking, so she waited for him to clarify.

"If Jindal is involved, it'll taint my sister's and nephew's life." He still refused to consider the possibility of Vandana being involved. "If this is something related to my childhood, my mother will blame herself."

"Anything will be better than them seeing you dead."

He chuckled and turned towards her. "You have an amazing knack of driving a point home."

"Did it work?"

Looking solemnly at her, he pulled her to him and kissed her. She responded with equal fervor, her body hungry for his after that night.

"Let's go to my room," he whispered against her lips, as his hands pulled at her shirt tucked at the waistband.

"Lots of work here. Have to study the phone logs once more." She pushed him back, worried by the findings and tension of the investigations.

"Give it a rest. You have been at it for the past three days, not to mention the nights."

"Sooner the better." The sentence brought with it the realization that she'd have to leave after the culprits were behind the bars. She stepped back with a fresh resolve of getting back to the status quo, sure that she would never be able to fit into his world.

Sensing her withdrawal, he released her and switched to his professional avatar. Sitting behind the desk, he took a full update on the investigation. In the end, he called up his mother and requested her to come there whenever she was free.

Asking Esha to call him when his mother arrived, he went up to his room to catch up on his own work, leaving her restless and edgy, wallowing in her own emotional conflict.

SETHS' RESIDENCE, MUMBAI
3RD NOVEMBER, 1:OO PM

"What is it Esha? Let's get over with it fast, I have to go to—" Mrs. Seth froze as she saw the crime board. "Why do you have *daija's* photo here on the board? And who is the—" She staggered back when she saw the picture of the trio.

Esha rushed to support her and eased her onto the sofa. She handed Mrs. Seth a glass of water and called Vikram over the intercom.

Mrs. Seth sat sipping the water at regular intervals, keeping her eyes averted from the crime board.

"Are you okay?" Vikram asked the moment he entered, crouching beside the sofa. "Do you recognize anyone from the picture?"

She sighed and nodded, then closed her eyes.

"Do you want to discuss this now? We can do it later, whenever you feel up to it."

"No, no sweetheart. If it is related to that scum who is out there with a gun pointed at your heart, I'd rather do it now."

Esha mentally applauded the woman for her strength and objectivity.

Vikram patted her shoulder, as Meera Seth took a deep breath again and began, "That woman in the center worked for your father as a junior secretary and..." she threw half a glance at Vikram and Esha, then continued, "...and your father had an affair with her. I got to know about it and had a huge row with your father. She was sent packing immediately after."

Vikram frowned, staring at the woman in the picture.

"What's her name? When was this?" Esha asked when she saw a speechless Vikram reeling with the impact of what he had heard.

"Saraswati Negi. This was before Vandana was born."

"Negi! Thirty-eight years!" Esha couldn't help but say it out loud. This didn't make sense. "The surname matches with the man. He could be her younger brother. We can get her personal information from the official records, but... Mrs. Seth, were you aware of any of her family members or where she had gone?"

"No. I haven't heard from her in so many years. Oh my God, is she taking revenge? From me? After so many years? Oh God... your father's name... our family name... it'll be all over in the newspapers!"

"Calm down, Mrs. Seth." Esha crouched in front of her. "We won't let the media get a whiff on it. But do you remember anything else? Any minute detail... anything will help."

"Stop tormenting her, Esha." Vikram took his mother's hand between his. "Don't worry, mom. We'll handle this. It's okay. Just relax. No one gets to know, I'll make sure." He took her to the family's rooms upstairs.

Esha glanced at the photo again and added one more event to the timeline. Thirty-eight years! The span of events didn't make any sense to her, assuming that they were in this together. So the woman was ditched in year zero and they had tried to kidnap Vikram after fifteen years, when he was nine. Here the question was why him? Why not Vandana? She wrote the question on the board.

After this, Vikram went to the US. Assuming that the trekking incident with Nikhil was not an accident, the first attack happened when he was twenty-seven, the second attack happened in Delhi after five years, and the third happened in Mumbai, soon after the attack in Delhi. While the first one was made to look like an accident, the other two were blatant assassination attempts. They were or he was getting desperate. He no longer cared for himself.

But why only Vikram? Why not Vandana?

The landline rang displaying Uday's number on the screen. She picked up the phone.

"Oh no. Goddamn."

"What happened?" Vikram entered the room.

"Daija is missing. Uday has raised an all point lookout for both of them."

He pursed his lips and raked his hand through his hair. "I have to go to the office tomorrow."

"Why?"

"I need a file from the office safe."

"I'll bring it."

"No."

"Can't you ask Koel to bring it?"

"No, she doesn't have the code," he said.

"But you can't go. The old woman has gone underground. They must have sensed something."

"For the same reason, you can't go too either."

"Come on... it's my job, I'm one of the PAs. They don't know about me."

Raking his hair with his finger, he exhaled. "Okay fine, but take Jay and the guards with you."

"I'll take only Jay and Uday's man stationed outside. More than that will arouse suspicion."

"What the hell! Okay fine." He touched her hair. "Be careful."

November 4th

SETH TOWERS, MUMBAI
4TH NOVEMBER, 11:30 AM

"Oh, you are here! To work? I thought you are earning your salary by warming his bed," Koel said the moment Esha entered the office. "I can't understand what he sees in you. Emaciated, ugly bitch." She continued her tirade as Esha stepped into Vikram's office.

Koel looked a little dull and dejected—maybe she was missing Vikram. Ruthlessly putting Koel and her disposition out of her mind, Esha entered the digits on the electronic panel of the safe and found the file. Closing the door, she smelled something sweet and turned to find Koel standing right in front of her.

Koel lifted her hand, on a reflex Esha grabbed her wrist twisted it towards her face. Koel gasped. The next second, Esha felt something move behind her, but before she could react someone hit her from behind and she collapsed in a dead faint.

SETHS' RESIDENCE, MUMBAI
4TH NOVEMBER, 2:45 PM

Vikram looked at the time when his mother entered his office with lunch on a tray. 'Esha should have been back by now.'

"You should eat, Vikram. You didn't even come down for breakfast." Mom kept the tray on the coffee table.

"You shouldn't have bothered, mom. Did you eat?" He glanced at the phone for any message. The unidentified unease which had shadowed his mind since Nikhil's accident was intensifying with every passing second.

"I'll eat with you. Kishore is taking care of Uday and his team in the kitchen."

Vikram picked up the phone and dialed Esha's number. The phone kept ringing but she didn't answer.

"Come now. Have a bite, then work."

He kept the phone near him and sat down to eat. He had barely finished half when his phone rang. It was a video call from an unknown number. His phone was wired to trace any call since the time he had been holed up at home, so taking the call was not a problem.

Frowning, he blocked his video and swiped to take the call.

"What the fuck!" The image had him stand up and blood drained out of his head. Esha was lying on a cot with her eyes closed and blood dripping from her arm. The only thing which was keeping him from freaking out was that her chest rose and fell rhythmically.

"I have her, and she is alive as of now." The voice was gruff and stern, though he couldn't see the man.

'Call Uday!' He mimed looking at his mother showing her the video.

"Who is this?" He asked out loud, keeping anxiety away from his tone, even though his heart hammered in his chest.

"Never mind who I am. I have her and you will do exactly as I say. Don't act smart at any cost. One misstep and she dies."

"What do you want?" As he asked the question, Uday rushed to his office.

"What I want?" He chuckled, then dissolved into manic laughter. "Come here and I'll tell you."

"Where?"

"Quite amenable are we?"

Vikram's blood boiled at the tone and watching Esha lying helplessly and under the madman's control.

"Even though you have blocked your video, I know you are sweating, Seth. It's good that your mother is with you. I want her to sweat too, a lot. Wanted to have your father around too but never mind."

Vikram heard his mother gasp near the door.

"Now listen to me carefully. You come to this address, your minions must have traced the location by now. You have to come in your black car, without any driver or guard, without anyone trailing you. No gun, no phone, no camera or any surveillance equipment. I know it will take half an hour for you to reach me if you start, say in next five minutes. Listen to me carefully, Seth. If I see any one with you she dies, if I see a gun or camera on you she dies. And believe me the entire parameter of my house is under my watch. I'll know. And she… you know what will happen. Please give your phone to your mother, I'll call her again, so that she can see what happens to her son. You have thirty minutes." The phone went dead.

"Did you get the location?" Vikram threw the phone on the table and picked up the keys to the car.

"Yes," Uday said.

"No, Vikram. You can't go." Mom stood in front of him, with tears in her eyes.

"I have to go, mom. I won't be able to live if I don't go today. I have to see him and ask why."

"Vikram… I have to tell you something."

"Now is not the time, mom. Uday—"

"Vikram please." She held his sleeves.

"Nothing will happen, mom. I think I will convince him to surrender." He gently took her to the couch and sat her down.

"What?" he asked when Uday stepped up.

"You can't go blind like this, Vikram."

"I can and I will. I can't lose her the way I lost Nikhil, I can't afford to lose her."

"I'm not saying you don't go. Let me scope this location out. Let me plant my people. We'll go prepared."

"I don't have time didn't you hear what that mad man said. Thirty minutes or she dies."

"He needs you not her."

"Yeah, and he harms her and poofs, then? I will go. Do the preparation on the go. You have half an hour."

"Ok fine. At least wear a bullet-proof packet. He never said anything about that so I guess it's fine, and keep this in your sock." He gave a knife to him. "And we'll tape a gun to your shoulder. Take another gun in your pocket, he'll expect it and will ask you to hand it over. Then he won't get to the second one on your shoulder. And one more thing—"

"I don't have time." Vikram took the knife.

"Wear the jacket, and listen to me carefully. I will trail you in the surveillance van. Will find the frequency of his camera and audio. When I find them I will clone the surroundings and replay the same to him. The moment that happens my team and I will rush into the building. So you have to just stall him. Keep talking to him, keep him engaged as long as possible."

"Got that." Vikram hugged his crying mother, picked up the key, and left the house.

SUBURBS, MUMBAI
4TH NOVEMBER, 3:30 PM

It was cold.

The first thought that came to her mind as Esha gained consciousness was that she was cold and weak. The second thought brought in acute panic. She couldn't move! Though fully clothed, she was drenched with, what seemed like, water. And she couldn't move. Memories came rushing, overwhelming her senses. Koel! Goddamn! Fear made her stomach churn and her skin broke into painful goosebumps.

As her eyes focused on her surroundings, Esha found herself in a small, eight by eight room that had a single, narrow iron bed and a chair at the foot. A yellow glow emanated from the earthen lamp on the floor and the fire in the *havankund.*

The massive life-size black idol on the wall opposite to her and the *Mahakaali yantra* pattern on the floor didn't surprise her, but fear knotted her stomach as her gaze landed on the man clad in a loincloth, sitting cross-legged in front of the *havankund*. He muttered rhythmically under his breath as he put something in the fire at regular intervals. The pallor of his skin matched the fake skull garland around the deity's neck. Thank God she could make out that they were fake.

The flickering shadows from the crackling fire and the massive, sharp knife kept on the side of the pattern sent slivers of fear cascading down her toes.

Clamping down the feeling of doom, she concentrated on the room. Since when had she been lying here? There was not a single opening in the room through which she could make out the time of the day. Stark white walls and the crude cemented floor told her that someone who didn't have much skill in masonry had built it.

She was tied to an iron bed—she judged from the rods cold against her arm. Her left arm was tied to a crude wooden scale and jutted out from the bed. Taking a deep breath, she focused on the positives. She could move her fingers and toes, an action that ruled out any extensive injury. But her arms ached. The injured shoulder had become stiff and the left arm had a series of cuts. She craned her neck and spotted a brass vessel kept below her arm that collected the blood. Her blood!

Some cuts had stopped bleeding and blood had coagulated leaving ugly maroon welts, but some bled with varied speed. No wonder she felt weak. The bed squeaked as she struggled against the nylon ropes tying her.

The man opened his eyes and turned towards her. Recognition dawned. Shivam Negi looked older yet sturdier than he had in the photograph Uday had unearthed from the army records. Again, she wasn't surprised. Now that the moment of suspense was about to be over, she waited for the man to start the conversation.

He was to be feared, she had known the first time she had spotted him near the guard room. Of course, at that time she didn't know who he was. But now that she knew, it took all her willpower to mask her fear.

"Don't worry. He'll be coming soon. Your role will be over the moment he's here," he said smiling and poured something in the holy fire. The fire hissed and sputtered making the shadows dance on his face and all over the room.

"What's the point?" She hoped he didn't hear her heart drum.

"You'll know soon. Have patience. I've kept my patience for such a long time."

"Really? How long?"

He chuckled.

"How many years?"

"Inquisitive, aren't you?" He smiled, the expression more like a grimace. "Since the day he was born, of course. You didn't even exist then."

"What if he doesn't come? Why would he come for me?" Esha hoped Vikram called his bluff.

"Oh, he'll come. I know him too well. He'll come for any of his servants loyal to him. And you are more than that. You are not mere staff. I know. The attraction of flesh. He'll definitely come. I have sent him a sweet looking picture of yours and a message. And to his mother too. Wanted his father to witness this day when they'll lose their precious son, but the bastard died too soon and too easily. But the bitch will pay."

"Why?" she frowned. "Why him and not Vandana Seth?"

"Didn't madame tell you all? One conniving old woman our Mrs. Seth is."

He poured *ghee* in the *havankund,* the flames sputtered and rose higher.

"Why?" Esha asked again ignoring the theatrics.

He glanced at her and sneered.

"Vandana is our blood. Seth Sr. and my Sara's daughter."

"What! Who is Sara?"

"Quiet!" he screamed and picked up the knife. "Don't take her name with your filthy mouth."

Esha throat dried up as the blade glimmered in the glow of the fire.

"Vandana is family, our blood. My Sara's daughter," he clarified when she didn't say anything and kept the knife down.

The next second, it hit her. Sara was Saraswati Negi. Esha reeled with the revelation. Not in a million attempts would she have guessed this fact. And why did Mrs. Seth hide this information when she had identified Saraswati Negi?

"Madame was unable to have a child and Sara was pregnant with her husband's child." It seemed like he wanted to talk. Keeping the secret for such a long time, he wanted to be heard. "So she made a bargain with my innocent Sara. A one-sided bargain, where madame got her husband and a child, and Sara had to leave the city, never to return. All our hopes, aspirations, and poverty-free future died with Sara's one signature on that document." His eyes had a glazed look and his lips had curled. He was on a roll. "My Sara could never recover from the heartbreak. I had to leave school. Shubha had to work in houses like a maid. We had made our peace with that, thinking that at least Vandana will get everything. But then suddenly, the junior arrives and once again Vandana is sidelined, married off to that scum."

He picked up the knife and made another cut on her arm. Esha doubled up in pain and bit her lip, not giving him the satisfaction by screaming. Her blood trickled into the brass vessel that he had shifted under the fresh wound. She wanted to drift off into blissful sleep again. But that was not a choice. To fight the pain and dizziness, she concentrated on his story.

"Was that the reason you kidnapped him first?"

"Yes, I didn't want to kill an innocent child."

"Then you tried to kill him during his trek since he was an adult and Vandana was married?"

"You figured that out?" He raised his eyebrows, then smiled. "Admirable. Don't talk much woman and surrender to the divine."

The next moment, Esha heard Vikram's voice over the speakers. Her heart drummed into different fear-inducing beats. A moment later, Vikram's face appeared over the monitor.

'*No, no, no.*' Esha shook her head to focus clearly. Why did Vikram come here? Didn't Uday drill some sense into him? He was playing into the hands of this madman.

"Oh, he is here," Negi squealed. "Wonderful."

He went to the microphone. "Vikramaditya Jr., I see you. Welcome to my humble abode. Remember I have eyes on you. No one else approaches the door or your sweetheart dies," he said, then cackled. He flicked a switch. "Now open the door, step inside, and close the door. No one else approaches the door or the whole house blows up," he repeated.

'*No, no, no.*' Against her wish, Esha saw Vikram follow the instructions.

Negi pressed the switch again. "Very good, now keep the gun and all the arms that you have in that basket at the beginning of the stairs and come down. Oh, by the way mind your head!" He laughed again uproariously at his own joke.

A few minutes later, Vikram appeared in the doorway. He gasped when he saw her on the iron bench and took a step towards her. "What the hell!"

"No, no... stop right there." Negi waved his gun. "You can't touch her. I have purified her, she is for the divine. Sit down on that chair."

"Vikram, you moron." She struggled feebly against her shackles, wanting to stand with Vikram, stand in front of him—it was her place, her duty. Nikhil would have been so disappointed.

"What the hell have you done to her?" Vikram snarled and stepped forward.

Negi placed a gun on Esha's temple. "I can shoot her right now if you don't cooperate."

The threat froze Vikram where he was, and his hands fisted by his side. "You are surrounded from all sides. You know you can't escape."

"Do you think we care?" *daija* said appearing in the doorway.

Esha closed her eyes. Great, the team was complete. They were going to die along with the madman and the old woman, Esha was sure. She desperately tried to find a weak knot, but couldn't. She was losing consciousness even though the blood had reduced to a trickle from the fresh gash on the arm. She forced her eyes to open and think of some way to save their lives.

"You are going to drop the gun and we'll not press any charges," Vikram said.

Negi hollered like a maniac and kept laughing.

"Do you think the police, arrest, charges matter?" he shouted suddenly. "Do you even have any idea what your father and mother did to Sara... to us?"

"Who is Sara? What have my parents done?"

"Shut up and stand back. Don't take Sara's name like that. She is Saraswati for you... a Goddess, a pure soul." Negi poked the gun at Esha's temple and Vikram sat down on the chair.

Esha gave up all hope of coming out alive from the room.

"Aditya?"

The stern yet soft voice jerked Esha awake from the faint she was sinking into. Esha's unusually calm heart began hammering again to see an old woman standing at the end of the stairs with Vikram's gun in her hand. With grey hair hanging down her shoulders, she looked like a doll who had aged in the tattered pink *salwar* suit. A smile broke on her face as she looked at Vikram. Hope glimmered in the dim room.

"Aditya," the old woman repeated taking a step towards Vikram.

"Sara, what are you doing here? How did you come here? From where did you get the gun?" Negi shouted.

"What are you doing to Aditya?"

"He is not Aditya," Negi said. "How the hell did you come on this side? Oh, the cupboard latch... I forgot to fix it... hell!"

"How dare you threaten my Aditya?"

"He is not Aditya! Can't you see?" Negi shouted.

"Silence," Sara shouted. In the excitement, her hand shook and she fired the gun. The bullet wheezed past Negi's ear and ricocheted off the wall behind, chipping the concrete. Looking daggers at him, she stood in front of Vikram, where Esha wanted to be—like a shield, his bodyguard.

"No one threatens my Aditya. He is the King. It's treason. You should bow to him," she said pointing the gun at Negi.

"Sara... darling, he is not Seth senior. He is his son," *daija* placated.

"His son? Meera can't bear children." Sara looked confused. "She is good just for maintaining a facade for the public. Aditya and I have a daughter. He has only ONE daughter. Stay where you are." Sara waved the gun at *daija,* as she took a step towards Sara.

"Look at what they have done to her. Your father duped her. She kept him on a pedestal and he cheated on her. And then, your mother took her child away," *daija* hissed.

"No, Anna is sleeping in her crib," Sara interrupted and pointed the gun again at Negi.

"They took away her only hope to live." *Daija* turned towards Esha. "They thought they were doing her a favor. They felt magnanimous. Look at me... I am so great that I have accepted my husband's love-child." *Daija* spat years of venom for Mrs. Seth, trying to imitate her. "We wanted your father to witness this, but he croaked just like that. *Kaali Maa's* will." She lifted her hands up, then looked at Vikram. "But the way she had snatched my Sara's child, we'll take hers. *Kaali Maa* knows how hard we tried to do that from the day you were born, but we were poor and you have been lucky. Very lucky. But now that luck has no role to play. Today we'll get the divine justice. Sara, come here."

Daija tried to pull Sara away from Vikram.

"I want to be with Aditya," she struggled. As *daija* tried to take the gun, it went off and *daija* fell down clutching her stomach, her sari drenched with blood.

"Nooo..." Negi screamed.

"Stay there and bow," Sara again aimed the gun at him.

"Sara, I'm your brother!"

"Are you?" She peered at him. "No, you are lying. My Shiva will never harm my Aditya."

"Come on, give me the gun, good girl. Look Anna is crying, you should go upstairs."

"No, Aditya has come back and I want to talk to him. I knew he'll come. He never lies to me."

"Get away from him." Negi took a step forward.

Another shot reverberated in the small confined area making Negi stagger back. He was shot in the chest. The gun from his hand slipped to the ground. The surprise etched on his face even as he lay there unmoving.

"No one threatens my Aditya." Sara touched Vikram's cheek. "Aditya..." She let the gun fall on the floor. "You have come for me! I knew you will. I've waited so long for this day..."

So much for divine justice! Esha let her head fall on the cot. Relieved to see that the danger was over, she gave in to the blissful unconsciousness.

⟶•⟨◆⟩•⟵

BREACH CANDY HOSPITAL, MUMBAI
4TH NOVEMBER, 9:30 PM

The soothing green and white walls of the hospital's waiting room did nothing to calm the turmoil inside Vikram. The doctors had examined him and run all the possible tests and there were no external wounds for them to treat. He had come back from the ordeal unscathed, but he didn't know how to deal with the internal scars he had received at Negi's revelation.

He sighed when the attendant brought a cup of coffee for him. Sipping the lukewarm, sugary brew he strolled towards the examination room. He had refused to meet his mother or sister. It would have hurt them, but right then he was in no mood to indulge anyone. He had to clear his own thoughts before facing the world.

From the one way mirror of the examination room, he looked at the confused, old woman, who had saved him. She was still asking for his father. Was any human being capable of that kind of devotion to another? Vikram had always kept his father on a pedestal, but today his idol lay shattered at the feet of this woman. The frail, endearing woman, who was his sister's mother too! How could his parents hide such an important detail of their lives from them? How in hell's name would he break the news to Vandana *di*?

His musing was broken with arrival of the doctor who was treating Esha. "She is doing fine. A few stitches were required. Nothing to worry about. Lost a lot of blood, but rest is all she needs."

"Thank you, doctor. May I see her?"

"Yes, of course." The doctor took him to the post-operative observation room. "She is still under anesthesia. You'll be able to speak to her tomorrow morning. By that time she will be shifted to a proper room."

"Thanks. Please make sure she gets the best," Vikram said.

The doctor nodded and left Vikram alone with Esha. This was the second time she had been injured because of him. She looked pale against the white sheets, and helpless with all the tubes and medical paraphernalia attached to her. The thought brought the whole gory scene, in that lunatic's basement, alive again. The person trailing Koel was found dead in the office parking lot.

Esha moved her hand. His heart thudded in his chest, as he fought the urge to take her into his arms. He had come so close to losing her too. Nikhil's face appeared in front of his eyes intensifying the fear and loss once again.

Sheer waste of life!

He had to pay a heavy price, all because of something his father had done when he didn't even exist, and for his mother's passion for preserving family honor and looking after what was theirs. His logical brain forced him not to blame them. They probably did the best under the circumstances, but still...

It would take some time to come to terms with the reality.

A movement to his left forced him to look at the intruder. His mother stood in front of the first examination room, watching Sara. Vikram hardened his heart when he saw Meera Seth wilt as recognition dawned.

"Who would have thought you will meet her again?" Vikram drawled.

"Is she... she is...?"

"Yes. She is one life that you have ruined. Of course, father is more to be blamed, but you too had a part in this—"

"What are you saying?" she whirled towards him. "I didn't expect you to be so judgmental, that too without knowing the whole truth."

"I know everything. I used to wonder about Vandana *di* too, you know." He continued, for once not bothering to ease her anxiety. "Remember the conversation we had at Alibaug? The fleeting thought used to worry me about her anxiety and panic attacks, but I kept quiet... thinking it was one of nature's pranks or that Jindal was a worthless fellow who added to her stress. But now everything has fallen in place, every piece of the puzzle has found its place, and I have lost a dear friend and was on the verge of losing the love of—" He paused and swallowed as his mother's eyes welled up.

Cursing under his breath he went and sat on the steel bench. After a couple of minutes, his mother sat beside him too, crying softly.

Taking a deep breath he placed his hand around her shoulders and pulled her to him.

———◆———

Epilogue

He watched her standing on the balcony.

It was time for the next step.

She would not be an easy target. He had seen her in action, she was no simpering female. That was the reason he had come prepared for every scenario before putting her on the plane as per his boss's instructions.

With purposeful strides, he hurried towards the four-apartment block. No one was there to stop him or question him. It was a wedding venue, not everyone was supposed to know everyone. Her apartment lock had already been taken care of, by his team-mates present at the entrance in plain clothes. He too wore jeans and a white t-shirt trying to merge with sleepy relatives.

He didn't pause to look around and stopped only after reaching the balcony effectively shielding her from any peeping Tom behind. He had memorized the way to the small room at the back—her room with the tiny, stark balcony. She stood in the same pose staring at the moon. Her shoulders tensed as he stopped at the threshold. His breath seemed to stop as she turned around and looked at him.

"Jay! What? Is everything alright? How did you even enter the house? I had locked it myself."

"Ma'am you know us." He jangled the bunch of master keys.

She looked tired, which was not surprising. She had hardly slept for more than two hours a day since he had been watching her.

"Sir wants to talk to you and has asked you to come with me to the airport. He has only a few hours before he leaves Delhi."

"Oh... he wants that... is it?" A veiled screen of emotion made her eyes flicker and chase away the sleepiness, but she relaxed against the railings and crossed her arms. "Tell him I refused."

"My job is on the line, please ma'am. He is in a mood."

She kept staring at him.

Jay sighed, "Ma'am please!"

Goddamn! She looked at the pleading man and decided it would probably be best to meet the boss, and tie the loose end once and for all.

———◈◆◈◆◈———

IGI AIRPORT, NEW DELHI
4TH FEBRUARY, 1:15 AM

It had been two long months since Vikram had taken care of the furor caused by the Negi family. He had to use a significant amount of diplomacy and clout to keep the lid on Sara's identity and his involvement in putting her in a proper institution so that she lived comfortably for the rest of her life.

Surprisingly Vandana *di* took the news stoically and accepted the fact without showing any undue distress.

In fact, she was largely instrumental in settling Sara in the special needs facility. They had later come to know that *Daija* had been stealing *di's* jewelry to fund their nefarious intentions. But now was not the time to dwell on that episode, he thought as he saw the car coming on the tarmac. He had to fix another important part of his life.

She was driving. Like a maniac. There was no one else in the car. He grinned. The hectic day was getting better.

It was a sight to see her walking across the concrete in the light of the waning moon, hair blowing across her face in tandem with the light breeze of the sultry night. She had let the tresses grow—probably for the wedding—and tried to tame them by tucking them behind her ears, but they refused to heed her wish.

He smiled at the sight of her marching onto the plane. Boy, was she angry?

"So, Jay was right," he began the moment she entered his plane.

"How could you gate crash my sister's wedding?" she spat.

"I had never pegged you as the sneaky type," he said trying to overcome the urge to hug her.

She raised an eyebrow.

"You shouldn't have slipped away from the hospital... the way you did."

"I left a note." She scowled.

"A note! Two lines written haphazardly, for what we feel for each other. You even missed the period at the end of the sentence."

She sighed.

"I think there are some etiquettes on leaving your lo... em... leaving someone who cared... who..."

That got her attention, and a little blush rose near her ears.

"That too when he is so busy and had asked you to wait," he finished the sentence lamely. Gosh, he had never been so corny even when he was a teenager. "Then you changed your mobile number as if I won't be able to track you down. Adding insults to my invisible wounds."

"So you sent your guards to kidnap me!"

He grinned. "Anything to get your attention." He took a step forward, she took one back maintaining the distance.

"Afraid of me?" he taunted.

"Never." She stopped.

He was satisfied to see her chest rising and falling rapidly, like his own. Pulling her by the waist he planted his mouth on her lips. Her whole body shuddered against him and she responded.

Esha felt that she had come home. Vikram had seeped into her system like no other, but all kinds of doubts reared their head again. She couldn't become like Urvi or Vandana, heading business ventures and charity organizations. The thought threw ice-cold water over her raging hormones and she pushed at his chest. When that didn't work and he continued his assault on her lips, she stepped on his toes.

"Ah... what the hell, Major!"

"This isn't going to work. Oh, the plane is moving!" She rushed to the window.

Someone coughed.

She turned to find the steward standing at a respectable distance outside the cockpit.

"Sir, you both need to buckle up," he said, looking at something beyond Vikram's shoulder, hands behind his back.

"Yes, of course. Thanks, Chetan," Vikram said, placing a hand on her arm. "Come, sit. We need to talk."

She slapped at his hand. "What's going on? You were actually thinking of kidnapping me, Vikram? Stop the plane right now! Like NOW!"

"I'm sorry, ma'am. We have got the clearance, and if we stop now the pilot will land in jail," Chetan said with the same bland expression and stance. She was sure his brilliant boss had coached him.

"Major, come on. I'll drop you back if we do not reach a conclusion." Vikram sat down and patted the seat next to him.

"What conclusion? We do not have anything to talk about, goddamn!" She sat down. "I have a house full of guests for my sister's wedding."

"Not full. By afternoon, all of them are leaving. Don't worry. Jay will take care of them," he said.

"You have thought of everything. Have you?"

"I'm quite a strategist, but you know that already." He grinned.

She sighed and buckled herself in.

"What do you think of this?"

She sucked in her breath when she saw the ring in the velvet box. The platinum ring's base was shaped like a Golf Club with its stick curving all around. A solitaire nestled like a ball at the center of the club's face. It was simple and beautiful, more so if someone knew the story behind it.

"It'll not suit anyone in your family."

"Will you marry me, Esha?"

She looked at him. His eyes as earnest and somber as a child's making her heart melt like molten lava. Affection surged into her throat. Goddamn, how she adored him!

"Vikram, please. I won't be able to handle."

"Handle what?" He pulled at her hand and caressed the scars on her arm.

"Life. I can't bear to live with constant threats and danger."

"What nonsense. You feel this is going to repeat in anyway?"

"No. But I won't be able to bear..." her voice thickened. "If... if anything happened to you." Embarrassed by her emotional display, she looked out of the window.

"What if we live apart and then something happens to me? Will you be able to bear?"

Panic surfaced at the thought. She had never considered that possibility. She swallowed the bile rising in her throat and turned to him, he was still looking at her in the same way. He scanned her face and picked up her left hand.

"Vikram, please," she whispered hoarsely.

"Come on! You've handled everything that had been thrown your way the month you were in Mumbai with consummate aplomb. Why this sudden uncertainty?" He slipped the ring on her finger.

"I don't like parties, and functions and I can't stand putting on makeup."

He laughed out loud and said in between his breath. "Then don't. You don't have to attend any function if you don't want to. I'm asking you to marry me, not be my slave."

"I won't fit in with your family."

"This is all hogwash. And you are marrying me, not my family. You and I are a perfect fit, Major. In fact, we are more than that, we are like a bullet in the gun." He put his hand on her nape and kissed her. "Think of an intelligent excuse," he said in between the kisses and caresses.

"Mmm... okay." She kissed him back matching his fervor, even though the seat belt pinched at her waist. "I'll think of one tomorrow."

"Tomorrow is better." His hand sneaked onto her breasts.

She sighed against his lips.

"Esha?"

"Hmm..."

"Do you know I have a bed on this plane?" he said as her hand wandered to his thigh.

The sentence brought her back to Earth, not literally. She pushed at him unsuccessfully. "Vikram, This isn't going to work. What will I do with my time?"

"Why, you'll be my bodyguard."

GLOSSARY

Aahuti	: Mixture of various things (butter, camphor, rice, sesame etc) put in the ceremonial fire for worship
Baba	: Nickname for someone younger
Bali	: Sacrifice
Beta	: Son or affectionate way of calling anyone younger
Bhaisabh	: Elder brother
Chachiji	: Aunt on the father's side
Dada	: Elder brother, or giving respect to an elder
Daija	: Nanny
Didi/ Di	: Elder sister, or a mark of respect for any girl/woman
Ghee	: Clarified butter
Gora	: Fair
Gulab-jamun	: Indian sweet-meat/ dessert
Havankund	: The conical large bowl used for ceremonial fire for worship
Janeyu	: Sacred cotton thread worn by Hindus during worship
Jijaji	: Sister's husband
Kaali/Mahakaali	: Hindu deity
Karmabhoomi	: Work place
Khichdi	: Indian dish of lentils and rice cooked together

Mama	: Mother's brother
Methi-paratha	: Indian bread stuffed with fenugreek leaves
Pahari	: From the hill region, language
Pooja	: Worship
Panditji	: Priest
Pallu	: Loose end of the sari
Maa	: Mother
Marathi	: Indian language
Nagin	: Female Naga (snake)
Paratha/Roti	: Indian bread
Rudraksh	: Sanskrit word, It is a seed of certain trees traditionally used as prayer beads
Saab	: Sir
Salwar suit	: Indian dress for ladies
Tadka Daal	: Fried lentils
Yaar	: Buddy
Yantra	: a geometrical diagram, or any object, used as an aid to meditation
'Om Krim Kaaliaaye Namah'	: Mantra to invoke the blessings of Goddess Kaali

ACKNOWLEDGEMENTS

There are times when I think what's the need of writing an acknowledgement note. People, who know me, know that I am forever grateful for their help, motivation and encouragement. They don't need an external endorsement or proof of my sentiments.

But—there is always a 'but' to any argument :) —I have realized (I'm glad not too late) that I want to capture the nuanced feelings and emotions that are going through me as the book continues climb the Amazon bestseller chart and maintains its position in its genre.

So here I am writing the 'acknowledgement' for this close-to-my-heart novel; 'The Bodyguard' after one month as I hit the 'publish' button on Amazon KDP, and I hope my well-wishers will forgive me for this delay.

The story wouldn't have been possible without the priceless feedback from my beta-readers Neelesh Inamdaar, Preethi Venugopala and Ruchira Khanna.

I would like to thank Neelesh for his insightful evaluation of the manuscript. This story would not have been what it is without his hard hitting email which made me realize that exceeding readers expectations is of paramount importance than publishing a half-baked product for a contest. Neelesh, God must be watching over me the day I thought of you as my beta reader for both Jugnu and The Bodyguard and you agreed. I really thank you for taking out time from your busy schedule and showing me the mirror.

Experts say whatever is visible sells, and that has been proven true with my new release. Thank you Manoj

Vijayan for such a fabulous cover. You have captured the essence of the story so beautifully in just one frame.

Shantala, my last-minute goto morale-booster. If you have given a green signal to my story then I'm sure it'll be a sure success. Thank you Nikita, for coming to my rescue at the last moment.

Last but not the least, I would like to thank my Rock of Gibraltar, my friends; Adite, Upreet, Sue, Preethi, Saiswaroopa, Devika, Esha, Paromita, Rubina, and Sundari, who are always there to advise, encourage and motivate me to move forward in life.

And thank you my creator for being with me in everything I do.

Cheers!

AUTHOR'S NOTE

Thank you for reading 'The Bodyguard'. I hope you enjoyed the story as I relished writing it particularly Esha's character, who is not only tough but has shades of vulnerability too. She makes mistakes but still moves on. That's life isn't it!

Word of mouth is an author's best friend and much appreciated. If you enjoyed, please consider telling your friends and/or posting a short review on Amazon or Goodreads.

Thank you,

Ruchi Singh.

www.ruchisingh.com

Email: author.ruchisingh@gmail.com

Amazon: Author Page

Facebook: www.facebook.com/ruchisinghauthor

Twitter: @ruchiwriter